LOST IN THE WII

BY ELEANOR STREDDER

CHAPTER I.

IN ACLAND'S HUT.

The October sun was setting over a wild, wide waste of waving grass, growing dry and yellow in the autumn winds. The scarlet hips gleamed between the whitening blades wherever the pale pink roses of summer had shed their fragrant leaves.

But now the brief Indian summer was drawing to its close, and winter was coming down upon that vast Canadian plain with rapid strides. The wailing cry of the wild geese rang through the gathering stillness.

The driver of a rough Red River cart slapped the boy by his side upon the shoulder, and bade him look aloft at the swiftly-moving cloud of chattering beaks and waving wings.

For a moment or two the twilight sky was darkened, and the air was filled with the restless beat of countless pinions. The flight of the wild geese to the warmer south told the same story, of approaching snow, to the bluff carter. He muttered something about finding the cows which his young companion did not understand. The boy's eyes had travelled from the winged files of retreating geese to the vast expanse of sky and plain. The west was all aglow with myriad tints of gold and saffron and green, reflected back from many a gleaming lakelet and curving river, which shone like jewels on the broad breast of the grassy ocean. Where the dim sky-line faded into darkness the Touchwood Hills cast a blackness of shadow on the numerous thickets which fringed their sheltering slopes. Onward stole the darkness, while the prairie fires shot up in wavy lines, like giant fireworks.

Between the fire-flash and the dying sun the boy's quick eye was aware of the long winding course of the great trail to the north. It was a comfort to perceive it in the midst of such utter loneliness; for if men had come and gone, they had left no other record behind them. He seemed to feel the stillness of an unbroken solitude, and to hear the silence that was brooding over lake and thicket, hill and waste alike.

He turned to his companion. "Forgill," he asked, in a low venturing tone, "can you find your way in the dark?"

He was answered by a low, short laugh, too expressive of contempt to suffer him to repeat his question.

3

One broad flash of crimson light yet lingered along the western sky, and the evening star gleamed out upon the shadowy earth, which the night was hugging to itself closer and closer every moment.

Still the cart rumbled on. It was wending now by the banks of a nameless river, where the pale, faint star-shine reflected in its watery depths gave back dim visions of inverted trees in wavering, uncertain lines.

"How far are we now from Acland's Hut?" asked the boy, disguising his impatience to reach their journey's end in careless tones.

"Acland's Hut," repeated the driver; "why, it is close at hand."

The horse confirmed this welcome piece of intelligence by a joyous neigh to his companion, who was following in the rear. A Canadian always travels with two horses, which he drives by turns. The horses themselves enter into the arrangement so well that there is no trouble about it. The loose horse follows his master like a dog, and trots up when the cart comes to a standstill, to take the collar warm from his companion's shoulders.

But for once the loose pony had galloped past them in the darkness, and was already whinnying at the well-known gate of Acland's Hut.

The driver put his hand to his mouth and gave a shout, which seemed to echo far and wide over the silent prairie. It was answered by a chorus of barking from the many dogs about the farm. A lantern gleamed through the darkness, and friendly voices shouted in reply. Another bend in the river brought them face to face with the rough, white gate of Acland's Hut. Behind lay the low farm-house, with its log-built walls and roof of clay. Already the door stood wide, and the cheerful blaze from the pine-logs burning on the ample hearth within told of the hospitable welcome awaiting the travellers.

An unseen hand undid the creaking gate, and a gruff voice from the darkness exchanged a hearty "All right" with Forgill. The lantern seemed to dance before the horse's head, as he drew up beneath the solitary tree which had been left for a hen-roost in the centre of the enclosure.

Forgill jumped down. He gave a helping hand to his boy companion, observing, "There is your aunt watching for you at the open door. Go and make friends; you won't be strangers long."

"Have you got the child, Forgill?" asked an anxious woman's voice.

An old Frenchman, who fulfilled the double office of man and maid at

4

Acland's Hut, walked up to the cart and held out his arms to receive the expected visitor.

Down leaped the boy, altogether disdaining the over-attention of the farming man. Then he heard Forgill whisper, "It isn't the little girl she expected, it is this here boy; but I have brought him all the same."

This piece of intelligence was received with a low chuckle, and all three of the men became suddenly intent upon the buckles of the harness, leaving aunt and nephew to rectify the little mistake which had clearly arisen—not that they had anything to do with it.

"Come in," said the aunt in kindly tones, scarcely knowing whether it was a boy or a girl that she was welcoming. But when the rough deer-skin in which Forgill had enveloped his charge as the night drew on was thrown aside, the look which spread over her face was akin to consternation, as she asked his name and heard the prompt reply, "Wilfred Acland; and are you my own Aunt Miriam? How is my uncle?" But question was exchanged for question with exceeding rapidity. Then remembering the boy's long journey, Aunt Miriam drew a three-legged stool in front of the blazing fire, and bade him be seated.

The owner of Acland's Hut was an aged man, the eldest of a large family, while Wilfred's father was the youngest. They had been separated from each other in early life; the brotherly tie between them was loosely knitted. Intervals of several years' duration occurred in their correspondence, and many a kindly-worded epistle failed to reach its destination; for the adventurous daring of the elder brother led him again and again to sell his holding, and push his way still farther west. He loved the ring of the woodman's axe, the felling and the clearing. He grew rich from the abundant yield of the virgin soil, and his ever-increasing droves of cattle grew fat and fine in the grassy sea which surrounded his homestead. All went well until his life of arduous toil brought on an attack of rheumatic fever, which had left him a bedridden old man. Everything now depended upon the energy of his sole surviving sister, who had shared his fortunes.

Aunt Miriam retained a more affectionate remembrance of Wilfred's father, who had been her playmate. When the letter arrived announcing his death she was plunged in despondency. The letter had been sent from place to place, and was nine months after date before it reached Acland's Hut, on the verge of the lonely prairie between the Qu'appelle and South Saskatchewan rivers. The letter was written by a Mr. Cromer, who promised to take care of the child the late Mr. Acland had left, until he

5

heard from the uncle he was addressing.

The brother and sister at Acland's Hut at once started the most capable man on their farm to purchase their winter stores and fetch the orphan child. Aunt Miriam looked back to the old letters to ascertain its age. In one of them the father rejoiced over the birth of a son; in another he spoke of a little daughter, named after herself; a third, which lamented the death of his wife, told also of the loss of a child—which, it did not say. Aunt Miriam, with a natural partiality for her namesake, decided, as she re-read the brief letter, that it must be the girl who was living; for it was then a baby, and every one would have called it "the baby." By using the word "child," the poor father must have referred to the eldest, the boy.

"Ah! very likely," answered her brother, who had no secret preference to bias his expectations. So the conjecture came to be regarded as a certainty, until Wilfred shook off the deer-skin and stood before his aunt, a strong hearty boy of thirteen summers, awkwardly shy, and alarmingly hungry.

But her welcome was not the less kindly, as she heaped his plate again and again. Wilfred was soon nodding over his supper in the very front of the blazing fire, basking in its genial warmth. But the delightful sense of comfort and enjoyment was rather shaken when he heard his aunt speaking in the inner room.

"Forgill has come back, Caleb; and after all it is the boy."

"The boy, God bless him! I only wish he were more of a man, to take my place," answered the dreamy voice of her sick brother, just rousing from his slumbers.

"Oh, but I am so disappointed!" retorted Aunt Miriam. "I had been looking forward to a dear little niece to cheer me through the winter. I felt so sure—"

"Now, now!" laughed the old man, "that is just where it is. If once you get an idea in your head, there it wedges to the exclusion of everything else. You like your own way, Miriam, but you cannot turn your wishes into a coach and six to override everything. You cannot turn him into a girl."

Wilfred burst out laughing, as he felt himself very unpromising material for the desired metamorphosis.

"How shall I keep him out of mischief when we are all shut in with the snow?" groaned Aunt Miriam.

"Let me look at him," said her brother, growing excited.

6

When Wilfred stood by the bedside, his uncle took the boy's warm hands in both his own and looked earnestly in his bright open face.

"He will do," murmured the old man, sinking back amongst his pillows. "There, be a good lad; mind what your aunt says to you, and make yourself at home."

While he was speaking all the light there was in the shadowy room shone full on Wilfred.

"He is like his father," observed Aunt Miriam.

"You need not tell me that," answered Caleb Acland, turning away his face.

"Could we ever keep him out of mischief?" she sighed.

Wilfred's merry laugh jarred on their ears. They forgot the lapse of time since his father's death, and wondered to find him so cheerful. Aunt and nephew were decidedly out of time, and out of time means out of tune, as Wilfred dimly felt, without divining the reason.

Morning showed him his new home in its brightest aspect. He was up early and out with Forgill and the dogs, busy in the long row of cattle-sheds which sheltered one end of the farm-house, whilst a well-planted orchard screened the other.

Wilfred was rejoicing in the clear air, the joyous sunshine, and the wonderful sense of freedom which seemed to pervade the place. The wind was whispering through the belt of firs at the back of the clearing where Forgill had built his hut, as he made his way through the long, tawny grass to gather the purple vetches and tall star-like asters, still to be found by the banks of the reed-fringed pool where Forgill was watering the horses.

Wilfred was intent upon propitiating his aunt, when he returned to the house with his autumn bouquet, and a large basket of eggs which Forgill had intrusted to his care.

Wilfred rushed into the kitchen, elate with his morning ramble, and quite regardless of the long trail of muddy footsteps with which he was soiling the freshly-cleaned floor.

"Look!" cried Aunt Miriam; but she spoke to deaf ears, for Wilfred's attention was suddenly absorbed by the appearance of a stranger at the gate. His horse and gun proclaimed him an early visitor. His jaunty air and the glittering beads and many tassels which adorned his riding-boots made Wilfred wonder who he was. He set his basket on the ground, and was

7

darting off again to open the gate, when Aunt Miriam, finding her remonstrances vain, leaned across the table on which she was arranging the family breakfast and caught him by the arm. Wilfred was going so fast that the sudden stoppage upset his equilibrium; down he went, smash into the basket of eggs. Out flew one-half in a frantic dance, while the mangled remains of the other streamed across the floor.

"Oh! the eggs, the eggs!" exclaimed Wilfred.

Aunt Miriam, who was on the other side of the table when he came in, had not noticed the basket he was carrying. She held up her hands in dismay, exclaiming, "I am afraid, Wilfred, you are one of the most aggravating boys that ever walked this earth."

For the frost was coming, and eggs were growing scarce.

"And so, auntie, since you can't transform me, you have abased me utterly. I humbly beg your pardon from the very dust, and lay my poor bruised offering at your indignant feet. I thought the coach and six was coming over me, I did indeed!" exclaimed Wilfred.

"Get up" reiterated Aunt Miriam angrily, her vexation heightened by the burst of laughter which greeted her ears from the open door, where the stranger now stood shaking with merriment at the ridiculous scene.

"Yes, off with you, you young beggar!" he repeated, stepping aside good-naturedly to let Wilfred pass. For what could a fellow do but go in such disastrous circumstances?

"It is not to be expected that the missis will put up with this sort of game," remarked Pêtre Fleurie, as he passed him.

Wilfred began to think it better to forego his breakfast than face his indignant aunt. What did she care for the handful of weeds? The mud he had gone through to get them had caused all the mischief. Everywhere else the ground was dry and crisp with the morning frost. "What an unlucky dog I am!" thought Wilfred dolefully. "Haven't I made a bad beginning, and I never meant to." He crept under the orchard railing to hide himself in his repentance and keep out of everybody's way.

But it was not the weather for standing still, and he longed for something to do. He took to running in and out amongst the now almost leafless fruit-trees to keep himself warm.

Forgill, who was at work in the court putting the meat-stage in order, looked down into the orchard from the top of the ladder on which he was mounted, and called to Wilfred to come and help him.

It was a very busy time on the farm. Marley, the other labourer, who was Forgill's chum in the little hut in the corner, was away in the prairie looking up the cows, which had been turned loose in the early summer to get their own living, and must now be brought in and comfortably housed for the winter. Forgill had been away nearly a fortnight. Hands were short on the farm now the poor old master was laid aside. There was land to be sold all round them; but at present it was unoccupied, and the nearest settler was dozens of miles away. Their only neighbours were the roving hunters, who had no settled home, but wandered about like gipsies, living entirely by the chase and selling furs. They were partly descended from the old French settlers, and partly Indians. They were a careless, light-hearted, dashing set of fellows, who made plenty of money when skins were dear, and spent it almost as fast as it came. Uncle Caleb thought it prudent to keep on friendly terms with these roving neighbours, who were always ready to give him occasional help, as they were always well paid for it.

"There is one of these hunter fellows here now," said Forgill. "The missis is arranging with him to help me to get in the supply of meat for the winter."

The stage at which Forgill was hammering resembled the framework of a very high, long, narrow table, with four tall fir poles for its legs. Here the meat was to be laid, high up above the reach of the many animals, wild and tame. It would soon be frozen through and through as hard as a stone, and keep quite good until the spring thaws set in.

Wilfred was quickly on the top of the stage, enjoying the prospect, for the atmosphere in Canada is so clear that the eye can distinguish objects a very long way off. He had plenty of amusement watching the great buzzards and hawks, which are never long out of sight. He had entered a region where birds abounded. There were cries in the air above and the drumming note of the prairie-hen in the grass below. There were gray clouds of huge white pelicans flapping heavily along, and faster-flying strings of small white birds, looking like rows of pearls waving in the morning air. A moving band, also of snowy white, crossing the blue water of a distant lakelet, puzzled him a while, until it rose with a flutter and scream, and proved itself another flock of northern geese on wing for the south, just pausing on its way to drink.

Presently Wilfred was aware that Pêtre was at the foot of the ladder talking earnestly to Forgill. An unpleasant tingling in his cheek told the subject of their conversation. He turned his back towards them, not choosing to hear the remarks they might be making upon his escapade of the morning, until old Pêtre—or Pête as he was usually called, for somehow the "r" slipped out of his name on the English lips around him —raised his voice, protesting, "You and I know well how the black mud by the reed pool sticks like glue. Now, I say, put him on the little brown pony, and take him with you."

"Follow the hunt!" cried Wilfred, overjoyed. "Oh, may I, Forgill?"

CHAPTER II.

HUNTING THE BUFFALO.

The cloudy morning ended in a brilliant noon. Wilfred was in ecstasies when he found himself mounted on the sagacious Brownie, who had followed them like a dog on the preceding evening.

Aunt Miriam had consented to Pête's proposal with a thankfulness which led the hunter, Hugh Bowkett, to remark, as Wilfred trotted beside him, "Come, you young scamp! so you are altogether beyond petticoat government, are you?"

"That is not true," retorted Wilfred, "for I was never out of her Majesty's dominion for a single hour in my life."

It was a chance hit, for Bowkett had been over the frontier more than once, wintering among the Yankee roughs on the other side of the border, a proceeding which is synonymous in the North-West Dominion with "getting out of the way."

Bowkett was a handsome fellow, and a first-rate shot, who could accomplish the difficult task of hunting the long-eared, cunning moose-deer as well as a born Red Indian. Wilfred looked up at him with secret admiration. Not so Forgill, who owned to Pête there was no dependence on these half-and-half characters. But without Bowkett's help there would be no meat for the winter; and since the master had decided the boy was to go with them, there was nothing more to be said.

Aunt Miriam came to the gate, in her hood and cloak, to see them depart.

"Good-bye! good-bye, auntie!" shouted Wilfred. "I am awfully sorry about those eggs."

"Ah, you rogue! do you think I am going to believe you?" She laughed, shaking a warning finger at him; and so they parted, little dreaming of all that would happen before they met again.

Wilfred was equipped in an old, smoked deer-skin coat of his uncle's, and a fur cap with a flap falling like a cape on his neck, and ear-pieces which met under his chin. He was a tall boy of his age, and his uncle was a little, wiry man. The coat was not very much too long for him. It wrapped over famously in front, and was belted round the waist. Pête had filled the pockets with a good supply of biscuit, and one or two potatoes, which he thought Wilfred could roast for his supper in the ashes of the campfire. For the hunting-party expected to camp out in the open for a night or two, as the buffaloes they were in quest of were further to seek and harder to find every season.

Forgill had stuck a hunting-knife in Wilfred's belt, to console him for the want of a gun. The boy would have liked to carry a gun like the others, but on that point there was a resolute "No" all round.

As they left the belt of pine trees, and struck out into the vast, trackless sea of grass, Wilfred looked back to the light blue column of smoke from the farm-house chimney, and wistfully watched it curling upwards in the clear atmosphere, with a dash of regret that he had not yet made friends with his uncle, or recovered his place in Aunt Miriam's good graces. But it scarcely took off the edge of his delight.

Forgill was in the cart, which he hoped to bring back loaded with game. At the corner of the first bluff, as the hills in Canada are usually called, they encountered Bowkett's man with a string of horses, one of which he rode. There was a joyous blaze of sunshine glinting through the broad fringes of white pines which marked the course of the river, making redder the red stems of the Norwegians which sprang up here and there in vivid contrast. A light canoe of tawny birch-bark, with its painted prow, was threading a narrow passage by the side of a tiny eyot or islet, where the pine boughs seemed to meet high overhead. The hunters exchanged a shout of recognition with its skilful rower, ere a stately heron, with grand crimson eye and leaden wings, came slowly flapping down the stream intent on fishing. Then the little party wound their way by ripple-worn rocks, covered with mosses and lichens. At last, on one of the few bare spots on a distant hillside, some dark moving specks became visible. The hunt began in earnest. Away went the horsemen over the wide, open plain. Wilfred and the cart following more slowly, yet near enough to watch the change to the stealthy approach and the cautious outlook over the hill-top, where the hunter's practised eye had detected the buffalo.

11

"Keep close by me," said Forgill to his young companion, as they wound their way upwards, and reached the brow of the hill just in time to watch the wild charge upon the herd, which scattered in desperate flight, until the hindmost turned to bay upon his reckless pursuers, his shaggy head thrown up as he stood for a moment at gaze. With a whoop and a cheer, in which Wilfred could not help joining, Bowkett again gave chase, followed by his man Diomé. A snap shot rattled through the air. Forgill drew the cart aside to the safer shelter of a wooded copse, out of the line of the hunters. He knew the infuriated buffalo would shortly turn on his pursuers. The loose horses were racing after their companions, and Brownie was quivering with excitement.

"Hold hard!" cried Forgill, who saw the boy was longing to give the pony its head and follow suit. "Quiet, my lad," he continued. "None of us are up to that sort of work. It takes your breath to look at them."

The buffalo was wheeling round. Huge and unwieldy as the beast appeared, it changed its front with the rapidity of lightning. Then Bowkett backed his horse and fled. On the proud beast thundered, with lowered eyes flashing furiously under its shaggy brows. A bullet from Diomé's gun struck him on the forehead. He only shook his haughty head and bellowed till the prairie rang; but his pace slackened as the answering cries of the retreating herd seemed to call him back. He was within a yard of Bowkett's horse, when round he swung as swiftly and suddenly as he had advanced. Wilfred stood up in his stirrups to watch him galloping after his companions, through a gap in a broken bluff at no great distance. Away went Bowkett and Diomé, urging on their horses with shout and spur.

"Halt a bit," said Forgill, restraining Wilfred and his pony, until they saw the two hunters slowly returning over the intervening ridge with panting horses. They greeted the approach of the cart with a hurrah of success, proposing, as they drew nearer, to halt for dinner in the shelter of the gap through which the buffalo had taken its way.

Wilfred was soon busy with Diomé gathering the dry branches last night's wind had broken to make a fire, whilst Bowkett and Forgill went forward with the cart to look for the fallen quarry.

It was the boy's first lesson in camping out, and he enjoyed it immensely, taking his turn at the frying-pan with such success that Diomé proposed to hand it over to his exclusive use for the rest of their expedition.

It was hard work to keep the impudent blue jays, with which the prairie abounded, from darting at the savoury fry, and pecking out the very middle of the steak, despite the near neighbourhood of smoke and flame, which threatened to singe their wings in the mad attempt.

But in spite of the thievish birds, dinner was eaten and appreciated in the midst of so much laughter and chaff that even Forgill unbent.

But a long day's work was yet before them, spurring over the sand-ridges and through the rustling grass. They had almost reached one of the westward jutting spurs of the Touchwood Hills, when the sun went down. As it neared the earth and sank amidst the glorious hues of emerald and gold, the dark horizon line became visible for a few brief instants across its blood-red face; but so distant did it seem, so very far away, the whole scene became dreamlike from its immensity.

"We've done, my lads!" shouted Bowkett; "we have about ended as glorious a day's sport as ever I had."

"Not yet," retorted Diomé. "Just listen." There was a trampling, snorting sound as of many cattle on the brink of a lakelet sheltering at the foot of the neighbouring hills.

Were they not in the midst of what the early Canadian settlers used to call the Land of the Wild Cows? Those sounds proceeded from another herd coming down for its evening drink. On they crept with stealthy steps through bush and bulrush to get a nearer view in the bewildering shadows, which were growing darker and darker every moment.

"Stop! stop!" cried Forgill, hurrying forward, as the light yet lingering on the lake showed the familiar faces of his master's cows stooping down to reach the pale blue water at their feet. Yes, there they were, the truant herd Marley was endeavouring in vain to find.

Many a horned head was lifted at the sound of Forgill's well-known call. Away he went into the midst of the group, pointing out the great "A" he had branded deep in the thick hair on the left shoulder before he had turned them loose.

What was now to be done?

"Drive them home," said the careful Forgill, afraid of losing them again. But Bowkett was not willing to return.

Meanwhile Diomé and Wilfred were busy preparing for the night at the spot where they had halted, when the presence of the herd was first perceived. They had brought the horses down to the lake to water at a

13

sufficient distance from the cows not to disturb them. But one or two of the wanderers began to "moo," as if they partially recognized their former companions.

"They will follow me and the horses," pursued Forgill, who knew he could guide his way across the trackless prairie by the aid of the stars.

"If you come upon Marley," he said, "he can take my place in the cart, for he has most likely found the trail of the cows by this time; or if I cross his path, I shall leave him to drive home the herd and return. You will see one of us before morning."

"As you like," replied Bowkett, who knew he could do without either man provided he kept the cart. "You will probably see us back at the gate of Acland's Hut by to-morrow night; and if we do not bring you game enough, we must plan a second expedition when you have more leisure."

So it was settled between them.

Forgill hurried back to the camping place to get his supper before he started. Bowkett lingered behind, surveying the goodly herd, whilst vague schemes for combining the twofold advantages of hunter and farmer floated through his mind.

When he rejoined his companions he found them seated round a blazing fire, enjoying the boiling kettle of tea, the fried steak, and biscuit which composed their supper. The saddles were hung up on the branches of the nearest tree, and the skins and blankets which were to make their bed were already spread upon the pine brush which strewed the ground.

"Now, young 'un," said Forgill solemnly, "strikes me I had better keep you alongside anyhow."

"No, no," retorted Diomé. "The poor little fellow has been in the saddle all day, and he is dead asleep already; leave him under his blankets. He'll be right enough; must learn to rough it sooner or later."

Forgill, who had to be his own tailor and washer-woman, was lamenting over a rent in his sleeve, which he was endeavouring to stitch up. For a housewife, with its store of needles and thread, was never absent from his pocket.

His awkward attempts awakened the mirth of his companions.

"What, poor old boy! haven't you got a wife at home to do the stitching for you?" asked Diomé.

14

"When you have passed the last oak which grows on this side the Red River, are there a dozen English women in a thousand miles?" asked Forgill; and then he added, "The few there are are mostly real ladies, the wives of district governors and chief factors. A fellow must make up his mind to do for himself and rub through as he can."

"Unless he follows my father's example," put in Bowkett, "and chooses himself a faithful drudge from an Indian wigwam. He would want no other tailor or washerwoman, for there are no such diligent workers in the world. Look at that," he continued, pointing to his beautifully embroidered leggings, the work of his Indian relations.

"Pay a visit to our hunters' winter camp," added Diomé, "and we will show you what an old squaw can do to make home comfortable."

There was this difference between the men: Diomé who had been left by his French father to be brought up by his Indian mother, resembled her in many things; whilst Bowkett, whose father was English, despised his Indian mother, and tried to make himself more and more of an Englishman. This led him to cultivate the acquaintance with the Aclands.

"I am going to send your mistress a present," he said, "of a mantle woven of wild dogs' hair. It belonged to the daughter of an Indian chief from the Rocky Mountains. It has a fringe a foot deep, and is covered all over with embroidery. You will see then what a squaw can do."

Forgill did not seem over-pleased at this information.

"Are you talking of my Aunt Miriam?" asked Wilfred, opening his sleepy eyes.

"So you are thinking about her," returned Forgill. "That's right, my lad; for your aunt and uncle at Acland's Hut are the only kith and kin you have left, and they are quite ready to make much of you, and you can't make too much of them."

"You have overshot the mark there," laughed Bowkett; "rather think the missis was glad to be rid of the young plague on any terms."

Diomé pulled the blankets over Wilfred's head, and wished him a *bonne nuit* (good night).

When the boy roused up at last Forgill had long since departed, and Diomé, who had been the first to awaken, was vigorously clapping his hands to warm them, and was shouting, "*Lève! lève! lève!*" to his sleepy companions.

15

"Get up," interpreted Bowkett, who saw that Wilfred did not understand his companion's provincial French. Then suiting the action to the word, he crawled out from between the shafts of the cart, where he had passed the night, tossed off his blankets and gave himself a shake, dressing being no part of the morning performances during camping out in the Canadian wilds, as every one puts on all the clothing he has at going to bed, to keep himself warm through the night.

The fire was reduced to a smouldering ash-heap, and every leaf and twig around was sparkling with hoar-frost, for the frost had deepened in the night, and joints were stiff and limbs were aching. A run for a mile was Bowkett's remedy, and a look round for the horses, which had been turned loose, Canadian fashion, to get their supper where they could find it.

The first red beams of the rising sun were tinging the glassy surface of the lake when Bowkett came upon the scattered quadrupeds, and drove them, with Wilfred's assistance, down to its blue waters for their morning drink.

Diomé's shouts recalled them to their own breakfast. He was a man of many tongues, invariably scolding in French—especially the horses and dogs, who heeded it, he asserted, better than any other language except Esquimau—explaining in English, and coming out with the Indian "Caween" when discourse required an animated "no." "Caween," he reiterated now, as Bowkett asked, "Are we to dawdle about all day for these English cow-keepers?" For neither Forgill nor Marley had yet put in an appearance.

The breakfast was not hurried over. The fire was built up bigger than ever before they left, that its blackened remains might mark their camping place for days, if the farming men came after them.

Wilfred, who had buckled the saddle on Brownie, received a riding lesson, and then they started, Diomé driving the cart. Wilfred kept beside him at first, but growing bolder as his spirits rose, he trotted onward to exchange a word with Bowkett.

The sharp, frosty night seemed likely to be followed by a day of bright and mellow sunshine. The exhilarating morning breeze banished all thoughts of fear and care from the light-hearted trio; and when the tall white stems of the pines appeared to tremble in the mid-day mirage, Wilfred scampered hither and thither, as merry as the little gopher, or ground squirrel, that was gambolling across his path. But no large game had yet been sighted. Then all unexpectedly a solitary buffalo stalked majestically

16

across what was now the entrance to a valley, but what would become the bed of a rushing river when the ice was melting in the early spring.

Bowkett paused, looked to his rifle and saddle-girths, waved his arm to Wilfred to fall back, and with a shout that made the boy's heart leap dashed after it. Wilfred urged his Brownie up the bank, where he thought he could safely watch the chase and enjoy a repetition of the exciting scenes of yesterday.

Finding itself pursued, the buffalo doubled. On it came, tearing up the ground in its course, and seeming to shake the quivering trees with its mighty bellow. Brownie plunged and reared, and Wilfred was flung backwards, a senseless heap at the foot of the steep bank.

CHAPTER III.

THE FIRST SNOWSTORM.

IN the midst of the danger and excitement of the chase, Bowkett had not a thought to spare for Wilfred. He and Diomé were far too busy to even wonder what had become of him. It was not until their work was done, and the proverbial hunger of the hunter urged them to prepare for dinner, that the question arose.

"Where on earth is that young scoundrel of a boy? Has he fallen back so far that it will take him all day to recover ground?" asked Bowkett.

"And if it is so," remarked Diomé, "he has only to give that cunning little brute its head. It is safe to follow the track of the cart-wheel, and bring him in for the glorious teasing that is waiting to sugar his tea."

"Rare seasoning for the frying-pan," retorted Bowkett, as he lit his pipe, and proposed to halt a bit longer until the truant turned up.

"Maybe," suggested Diomé, "if May bees fly in October, that moose-eared pony [the long ears of the moose detect the faintest sound at an inconceivable distance] has been more than a match for his raw equestrianism. It has heard the jog-trot of that solemn and sober cowherd, and galloped him off to join his old companions. What will become of the scattered flock?"

"Without a leader," put in Bowkett. "I have a great mind to bid for the office."

"Oh, oh!" laughed Diomé. "I have something of the keen scent of my Indian grandfather; I began to sniff the wind when that mantle was talked about last night. Now then, are we going to track back to find this boy?"

"I do not know where you propose to look for him, but I can tell you where you will find him—munching cakes on his auntie's lap. We may as well save time by looking in the likeliest place first," retorted Bowkett.

The bivouac over, they returned to Acland's Hut with their well-laden cart, and Wilfred was left behind them, no one knew where. The hunters' careless conclusions were roughly shaken, when they saw a riderless pony trotting leisurely after them to the well-known door. Old Pête came out and caught it by the bridle. An ever-rising wave of consternation was spreading. No one as yet had put it into words, until Forgill emerged from the cattle-sheds with a sack on his shoulder, exclaiming, "Where's the boy?"

"With you, is not he? He did not say much to us; either he or his pony started off to follow you. He was an unruly one, you know," replied Bowkett. Forgill's only answer was a hoarse shout to Marley, who had returned from his wanderings earlier in the day, to come with torches. Diomé joined them in the search.

Bowkett stepped into the house to allay Aunt Miriam's fears with his regret the boy had somehow given them the slip, but Forgill and Diomé had gone back for him.

An abundant and what seemed to them a luxuriant supper had been provided for the hunting party. Whilst Bowkett sat down to enjoy it to his heart's content, Aunt Miriam wandered restlessly from room to room, cautiously breaking the ill news to her brother, by telling him only half the hunting party had yet turned up. Pête was watching for the stragglers.

He roused himself up to ask her who was missing.

But her guarded reply reassured him, and he settled back to sleep. Such mishaps were of every-day occurrence.

"A cold night for camping out," he murmured. "You will see them with the daylight."

But the chilly hour which precedes the dawn brought with it a heavy fall of snow.

Aunt Miriam's heart sank like lead, for she knew that every track would be obliterated now. Bowkett still laughed away her fears. Find the boy they would, benumbed perhaps at the foot of a tree, or huddled up in some sheltering hollow.

18

Then Aunt Miriam asked Bowkett if he would earn her everlasting gratitude, by taking the dogs and Pête, with skins and blankets—

"And bringing the truant home," responded Bowkett boastfully.

The farm-house, with its double doors and windows, its glowing stoves in every room, was as warm and cozy within as the night without was cheerless and cold. Bowkett, who had been enjoying his taste of true English comfort, felt its allurements enhanced by the force of the contrast. Aunt Miriam barred the door behind him with a great deal of unearned gratitude in her heart. Her confidence in Forgill was shaken. He ought not to have brought home the cows and left her nephew behind. Yet the herd was so valuable, and he felt himself responsible to his master for their well-being. She did not blame Forgill; she blamed herself for letting Wilfred go with him. She leaned upon the hunter's assurances, for she knew that his resource and daring, and his knowledge of the country, were far greater than that possessed by either of the farming men.

The storm which had burst at daybreak had shrouded all around in a dense white sheet of driving snowflakes. Even objects close at hand showed dim and indistinct in the gray snow-light. On the search-party went, groping their way through little clumps of stunted bushes, which frequently deceived them by a fancied resemblance to a boyish figure, now throwing up its arms to call attention, now huddled in a darkling heap. Their shouts received no answer: that went for little. The boy must long ago have succumbed to such a night without fire or shelter They felt among the bushes. The wet mass of snow struck icily cold on hands and faces. A bitter, biting wind swept down the river from the north-east, breaking the tall pine branches and uprooting many a sapling. The two search-parties found each other that was all. Such weather in itself makes many a man feel savage-tempered and sullen. If they spoke at all, it was to blame one another.

While thus they wandered to and fro over the hunting-ground of yesterday, where was the boy they failed to meet? Where was Wilfred? Fortunately for him the grass grew thick and tall at the bottom of the bank down which he had fallen. Lost to view amid the waving yellow tufts which had sprung up to giant size in the bed of the dried-up stream, he lay for some time in utter unconsciousness; whilst the frightened pony, finding itself free, galloped madly away over the sandy ridges they had been crossing earlier in the morning.

By slow degrees sight and sound returned to the luckless boy. He was bruised and shaken, and one ankle which he had bent under him made him cry out with pain when he tried to rise. At last he drew himself into a sitting posture and looked around. Recollections came back confusedly at first. As his ideas grew clearer, he began to realize what had happened. Overhead the sky was gloomy and dark. A stormy wind swept the whitened grass around him into billowy waves. Wilfred's first thought was to shout to his companions; but his voice was weak and faint, and a longing for a little water overcame him.

Finding himself unable to walk, he dropped down again in the grassy nest which he had formed for himself, and tried to think. The weight of his fall had crushed the grass beneath him into the soft clayey mud at the bottom of the valley. But the pain in his ankle predominated over every other consideration. His first attempt to help himself was to take the knife out of his belt and cut down some of the grass within reach, and make a softer bed on which to rest it. His limbs were stiffening with the cold, and whilst he had still feeling enough in his fingers to undo his boot, he determined to try to bind up his ankle. Whilst he held it pressed between both his hands it seemed easier.

But Wilfred knew he must not sit there waiting for Forgill, who, he felt sure, would come and look for him if he had rejoined the hunting party: if —there were so many *ifs* clinging to every thought Wilfred grew desperate. He grasped a great handful of the sticky clay and pressed it round his ankle in a stiff, firm band. There was a change in the atmosphere. In the morning that clay would have been hard and crisp with the frost, now it was yielding in his hand; surely the snow was coming. Boy as he was, he knew what that would do for him—he should be buried beneath it in the hole in which he lay. It roused him to the uttermost. Deep down in Wilfred's nature there was a vein of that cool daring which the great Napoleon called "two o'clock in the morning courage"—a feeling which rises highest in the face of danger, borrowing little from its surroundings, and holding only to its own.

"If," repeated Wilfred, as his thoughts ran on—"if they could not find me, and that is likely enough, am I going to lie here and die?"

He looked up straight into the leaden sky. "There is nothing between us and God's heaven," he thought. "It is we who see such a little way. He can send me help. It may be coming for what I know, one way or another. What is the use of sitting here thinking? Has Bowkett missed me? Will he turn back to look me up? Will Forgill come? If I fall asleep down in this grass, how could they see me? Any way, I must get out of this hole." He tore the lining out of his cap and knotted it round his ankle, to keep the clay in place; but to put his boot on again was an impossibility. Even he knew his toes would freeze before morning if he left them uncovered. He took his knife and cut off the fur edge down the front of the old skin coat, and wound his foot up in it as fast as he could. Then, dragging his boot along with him, he tried hard to crawl up the bank; but it was too steep for him, and he slipped back again, hurting himself a little more at every slide.

This, he told himself, was most unnecessary, as he was sore enough and stiff enough before. Another bad beginning. What was the use of stopping short at a bad beginning? He thought of Bruce and his spider. He had not tried seven times yet.

Wilfred's next attempt was to crawl towards the entrance of the valley— this was easier work. Then he remembered the biscuit in his pocket. It was not all gone yet. He drew himself up and began to eat it gladly enough, for he had had nothing since his breakfast. The biscuit was very hard, and he crunched it, making all the noise he could. It seemed a relief to make any sort of sound in that awful stillness.

He was growing almost cheery as he ate. "If I can only find the cart-track," he thought; "and I must be near it. Diomé was behind us when I was thrown; he must have driven past the end of this valley. If I could only climb a tree, I might see where the grass was crushed by the cart-wheel."

But this was just what Wilfred could not do. The last piece of biscuit was in his hand, when a dog leaped out of the bushes on the bank above him and flew at it. Wilfred seized his boot to defend himself; but that was hopeless work, crawling on the ground. It was a better thought to fling the biscuit to the dog, for if he enraged it—ah! it might tear him to pieces. It caught the welcome boon in its teeth, and devoured it, pawing the ground impatiently for more. Wilfred had but one potato left. He began to cut it in slices and toss them to the dog. A bright thought had struck him: this dog might have a master near. No doubt about that; and if he were only a wild Red Indian, he was yet a man. Full of this idea, Wilfred emptied out his pockets to see if a corner of biscuit was left at the bottom. There were plenty of crumbs. He forgot his own hunger, and held out his hand to the dog. It was evidently starving. It sat down before him, wagging its bushy tail and moving its jaws beseechingly, in a mute appeal for food. Wilfred

21

drew himself a little nearer, talking and coaxing. One sweep of the big tongue and the pile of crumbs had vanished.

There was a sound—a crashing, falling sound—in the distance. How they both listened! Off rushed the furry stranger.

"It is my chance," thought Wilfred, "my only chance."

He picked up the half-eaten potato and scrambled after the dog, quite forgetting his pain in his desperation. A vociferous barking in the distance urged him on.

It was not Bowkett, by the strange dog; but another hunting party might be near. The noise he had heard was the fall of some big game. Hope rose high; but he soon found himself obliged to rest, and then he shouted with all his might. He was making his way up the valley now. He saw before him a clump of willows, whose drooping boughs must have lapped the stream. His boot was too precious to be left behind; he slung it to his belt, and then crawled on. One more effort. He had caught the nearest bough, and, by its help, he drew himself upright. Oh the pain in the poor foot when he let it touch the ground! it made him cry out again and again. Still he persisted in his purpose. He grasped a stronger stem arching higher overhead, and swung himself clear from the ground. The pliant willow swayed hither and thither in the stormy blast. Wilfred almost lost his hold. The evening shadows were gathering fast. The dead leaves swept down upon him with every gust. The wind wailed and sighed amongst the tall white grass and the bulrushes at his feet. It was impossible to resist a feeling of utter desolation.

Wilfred shut his eyes upon the dreary scene. The snatch of prayer on his lips brought back the bold spirit of an hour ago. He rested the poor injured ankle on his other foot, and drew himself up, hand over hand, higher and higher, to the topmost bough, and there he clung, until a stronger blast than ever flung him backwards towards the bank. He felt the bough giving way beneath his weight, and, with a desperate spring, clutched at the stunted bushes which had scratched his cheek when for one moment, in the toss of the gale, he had touched the hard, firm, stony ridge. Another moment, and Wilfred found himself, gasping and breathless, on the higher ground. An uprooted tree came down with a shock of thunder, shaking the earth beneath him, loosening the water-washed stones, and crashing among the decaying branches of its fellow pines.

22

At last the whirl of dust and stones subsided, and the barking of the dog made itself heard once more above the roar of the gale. Trembling at his hair-breadth escape, Wilfred cleared the dust from his eyes and looked about him. A dark form was lying upon the shelving ground. He could just distinguish the outstretched limbs and branching antlers of a wild moose-deer.

Whoever the hunter might be he would seek his quarry. Wilfred felt himself saved. The tears swam before his eyes. He was looking upward in the intensity of his thankfulness. He did not see the arrow quivering still in the dead deer's flank, or he would have known that it could only have flown from some Indian bow.

He had nothing to do but to wait, to wait and shout. A warm touch on the tip of his ear made him look round; the dog had returned to him. It, too, had been struck—a similar arrow was sticking in the back of its neck. It twisted its head round as far as it was possible, vainly trying to reach it, and then looked at Wilfred with a mute, appealing glance there was no mistaking. The boy sat up, laid one hand on the dog's back, and grasped the arrow with the other. He tugged at it with all his might; the point was deep in the flesh. But it came out at last, followed by a gush of blood.

"Stand still, good dog. There, quiet, quiet!" cried Wilfred quickly, as he tore a bit of fur off his cap and plugged the hole.

The poor wounded fellow seemed to understand all about it. He only turned his head and licked the little bit of Wilfred's face that was just visible under his overwhelming cap. A doggie's gratitude is never wanting.

"Don't, you stupid," said Wilfred. "How am I to see what I am about if you keep washing me between my eyes? There! just what I expected, it is out again. Now, steady."

Another try, and the plug was in again, firmer than before.

"There, there! lie down, and let me hold it a bit," continued Wilfred, carefully considering his shaggy acquaintance.

He was a big, handsome fellow, with clean, strong legs and a hairy coat, which hung about his keen, bright eyes and almost concealed them. But the fur was worn and chafed around his neck and across his back, leaving no doubt in Wilfred's mind as to what he was.

"You have been driven in a sledge, old boy," he said, as he continued to fondle him. "You've worn harness until it has torn your coat and made it shabbier than mine. You are no hunter's dog, as I hoped. I expect you have been overdriven, lashed along until you dropped down in the traces; and then your hard-hearted driver undid your harness, and left you to live or die. Oh! I know their cruel ways. How long have you been wandering? It isn't in nature that I shouldn't feel for you, for I am afraid, old fellow, I am in for such another 'do.'"

Wilfred was not talking to deaf ears. The dog lay down beside him, and stretched its long paws across his knee, looking up in his face, as if a word of kindness were something so new, so unimagined, so utterly incomprehensible. Was it the first he had ever heard?

No sunset glory brightened the dreary scene. All around them was an ever-deepening gloom. Wilfred renewed his shouts at intervals, and the dog barked as if in answer. Then followed a long silent pause, when Wilfred listened as if his whole soul were in his ears. Was there the faintest echo of a sound? Who could distinguish in the teeth of the gale, still tearing away the yellow leaves from the storm-tossed branches, and scaring the wild fowl from marsh and lakelet? Who could tell? And yet there was a shadow thrown across the white pine stem.

Another desperate shout. Wilfred's heart was in his mouth as he strove to make himself heard above the roar of the wind. On came the stately figure of a wild Cree chief. His bow was in his hand, but he was glancing upwards at the stormy sky. His stealthy movements and his light and noiseless tread had been unheard, even by the dog.

The Indian was wearing the usual dress of the Cree—a coat of skin with a scarlet belt, and, as the night was cold, his raven elf-locks were covered with a little cap his squaw had manufactured from a rat-skin. His blue cloth leggings and beautiful embroidered moccasins were not so conspicuous in the fading light. Wilfred could but notice the fingerless deer-skin mittens covering the hand which grasped his bow. His knife and axe were stuck in his belt, from which his well-filled quiver hung.

Wilfred tumbled himself on to one knee, and holding out the arrow he had extracted from the dog, he pointed to the dead game on the bank.

Wilfred was more truly afraid of the wild-looking creature before him than he would have been of the living moose.

24

CHAPTER IV.

MAXICA, THE CREE INDIAN.

Wilfred thought his fears were only too well-founded when he saw the Indian lay an arrow on his bow-string and point it towards him. He had heard that Indians shoot high. Down he flung himself flat on his face, exclaiming, "Spare me! spare me! I'm nothing but a boy."

The dog growled savagely beside him.

Despite the crash of the storm the Indian's quick ear had detected the sound of a human voice, and his hand was stayed. He seemed groping about him, as if to find the speaker.

"I am here," shouted Wilfred, "and there is the moose your arrow has brought down."

The Indian pointed to his own swarthy face, saying with a grave dignity, "The day has gone from me. I know it no longer. In the dim, dim twilight which comes before the night I perceive the movement, but I no longer see the game. Yet I shoot, for the blind man must eat."

Wilfred turned upon his side, immensely comforted to hear himself answered in such intelligent English. He crawled a little nearer to the wild red man, and surveyed him earnestly as he tried to explain the disaster which had left him helpless in so desolate a spot. He knew he was in the hunting-grounds of the Crees, one of the most friendly of the Indian tribes. His being there gave no offence to the blind archer, for the Indians hold the earth is free to all.

The chief was wholly intent upon securing the moose Wilfred had told him his arrow had brought down.

"I have missed the running stream," he went on. "I felt the willow leaves, but the bed by which they are growing is a grassy slope."

"How could you know it?" asked Wilfred, in astonishment.

The Indian picked up a stone and threw it over the bank. "Listen," he said; "no splash, no gurgle, no water there." He stumbled against the fallen deer, and stooping down, felt it all over with evident rejoicing.

He had been medicine man and interpreter for his tribe before the blindness to which the Indians are so subject had overwhelmed him. It

25

arises from the long Canadian winter, the dazzling whiteness of the frozen snow, over which they roam for three parts of the year, which they only exchange for the choking smoke that usually fills their chimneyless wigwams.

The Cree was thinking now how best to secure his prize. He carefully gathered together the dry branches the storm was breaking and tearing away in every direction, and carefully covered it over. Then he took his axe from his belt and cut a gash in the bark of the nearest tree to mark the spot.

Wilfred sat watching every movement with a nervous excitement, which helped to keep his blood from freezing and his heart from failing.

The dog was walking cautiously round and round whilst this work was going forward.

The Cree turned to Wilfred.

"You are a boy of the Moka-manas?" (big knives, an Indian name for the white men).

"Yes," answered Wilfred.

When the *cache*, as the Canadians call such a place as the Indian was making, was finished, the darkness of night had fallen. Poor Wilfred sat clapping his hands, rubbing his knees, and hugging the dog to keep himself from freezing altogether. He could scarcely tell what his companion was about, but he heard the breaking of sticks and a steady sound of chopping and clearing. Suddenly a bright flame shot up in the murky midnight, and Wilfred saw before him a well-built pyramid of logs and branches, through which the fire was leaping and running until the whole mass became one steady blaze. Around the glowing heap the Indian had cleared away the thick carpet of pine brush and rubbish, banking it up in a circle as a defence from the cutting wind.

He invited Wilfred to join him, as he seated himself in front of the glowing fire, wrapped his bearskin round him, and lit his pipe.

The whole scene around them was changed as if by magic. The freezing chill, the unutterable loneliness had vanished. The ruddy light of the fire played and flickered among the shadowy trees, casting bright reflections of distorted forms along the whitening ground, and lighting up the cloudy sky with a radiance that must have been visible for miles. Wilfred was not slow in making his way into the charmed circle. He got over the ground like a worm, wriggling himself along until his feet were over the bank, and down he dropped in front of the glorious fire. He coiled himself round with a sense of exquisite enjoyment, stretching his stiffened limbs and spreading his hands to the glowing warmth, and altogether behaving in as senseless a fashion as the big doggie himself. He had waited for no invitation, bounding up to Wilfred in extravagant delight, and now lay rolling over and over before the fire, giving sharp, short barks of delight at the unexpected pleasure.

It was bliss, it was ecstasy, it was paradise, that sudden change from the bleak, dark, shivering night to the invigorating warmth and the cheery glow.

The Cree sat back in dreamy silence, sending great whiffs of smoke from the carved red-stone bowl of his long pipe, and watching the dog and the boy at play. Their presence in noways detracted from his Indian comfort, for the puppy and the pappoose are the Cree's delight by his wigwam fire.

Hunger and thirst were almost forgotten, until Wilfred remembered his potato, and began to busy himself with roasting it in the ashes. But the dog, mistaking his purpose, and considering it a most inappropriate gift to the fire, rolled it out again before it was half roasted, and munched it up with great gusto.

"There's a shame! you bad old greedy boy," exclaimed Wilfred, when he found out what the dog was eating. "Well," he philosophised, determined to make the best of what could not now be helped, "I had a breakfast, and you—why, you look as if you had had neither breakfast, dinner, nor supper for many a long day. How have you existed?"

But this question was answered before the night was out. The potato was hot, and the impatient dog burned his lips. After sundry shakings and rubbings of his nose in the earth, the sagacious old fellow jumped up the bank and ran off. When he returned, his tongue touched damp and cool, and there were great drops of water hanging in his hair. Up sprang the thirsty Wilfred to search for the spring. The Cree was nodding; but the boy had no fear of losing himself, with that glorious fire-shine shedding its radiance far and wide through the lonely night. He called the dog to follow him, and groped along the edge of the dried-up watercourse, sometimes on all fours, sometimes trying to take a step. Painful as it was, he was satisfied his foot was none the worse for a little movement. His effort was rewarded. He caught the echo of a trickling sound from a corner of rock jutting out of the stunted bushes. The dog, which seemed now to guess the object of his search, led him up to a breakage in the lichen-covered stone, through which a bubbling spring dashed its warm spray into their faces. Yes, it was warm; and when Wilfred stooped to catch the longed-for water in his hands, it was warm to his lips, with a strong disagreeable taste. No matter, it was water; it was life. It was more than simple water; he had lighted on a sulphur spring. Wilfred drank eagerly as he felt its tonic effects fortifying him against the benumbing cold. For the wind seemed cutting the skin from his face, and the snowflakes driving before the blast were changing the dog from black to white.

Much elated with his discovery, Wilfred returned to the fire, where the Cree still sat in statue-like repose.

"He is fast asleep," thought Wilfred, as he got down again as noiselessly as he could; but the Indian's sleep was like the sleep of the wild animal. Hearing was scarcely closed. He opened one eye, comprehended that it was Wilfred returning, and shut it, undisturbed by the whirling snow. Wilfred set up two great pieces of bark like a penthouse over his head, and coaxed the dog to nestle by his side. Sucking the tip of his beaver-skin gloves to still the craving for his supper, he too fell asleep, to awake shivering in the gray of the dawn to a changing world. Everywhere around him there was one vast dazzling whirl of driving sleet and dancing snow. The fire had become a smouldering pile, emitting a fitful visionary glow. On every side dim uncertain shapes loomed through the whitened atmosphere. A scene so weird and wild struck a chill to his heart. The dog moved by Wilfred's side, and threw off something of the damp, cold weight that was oppressing him. He sat upright.

Maxica, or Crow's Foot—for that was the Cree's name—was groping round and round the circle, pulling out pieces of dead wood from under the snow to replenish the dying fire. But he only succeeded in making it hiss and crackle and send up volumes of choking smoke, instead of the cheery flames of last night.

Between the dark, suffocating cloud which hovered over the fire and the white whirling maze beyond it, Maxica, with his failing sight, was completely bewildered. All tracks were long since buried and lost. It was equally impossible to find the footprints of Wilfred's hunting party, or to follow his own trail back to the birch-bark canoe which had been his home during the brief, bright summer. He folded his arms in hopeless, stony despair.

"We are in for a two days' snow," he said; "if the fire fails us and refuses to

28

burn, we are as good as lost."

The dog leaped out of the sunken circle, half-strangled with the smoke, and Wilfred was coughing. One thought possessed them both, to get back to the water. Snow or no snow, the dog would find it. The Cree yielded to Wilfred's entreaty not to part company.

"I'll be eyes for both," urged the boy, "if you will only hold my hand."

Maxica replied by catching him round the waist and carrying him under one arm. They were soon at the spring. It was gushing and bubbling through the snow which surrounded it, hot and stinging as before. The dog was lapping at the little rill ere it lost itself in the all-shrouding snow.

In another minute Wilfred and the Cree were bending down beside it. Wilfred was guiding the rough, red hand to the right spot; and as Maxica drank, he snatched a drop for himself.

To linger beside it seemed to Wilfred their wisest course, but Maxica knew the snow was falling so thick and fast they should soon be buried beneath it. The dog, however, did not share in their perplexity. Perhaps, like Maxica, he knew they must keep moving, for he dashed through the pathless waste, barking loudly to Wilfred to follow.

The snow was now a foot deep, at least, on the highest ground, and Wilfred could no longer make his way through it. Maxica had to lift him out of it again and again. At last he took him on his back, and from this unwonted elevation Wilfred commanded a better outlook. The dog was some way in advance, making short bounds across the snow and leaving a succession of holes behind him. He at least appeared to know where he was going, for he kept as straight a course as if he were following some beaten path.

But Maxica knew well no such path existed. Every now and then they paused at one of the holes their pioneer had made, to recover breath.

"How long will this go on?" thought Wilfred. "If Maxica tires and lays me down my fate is sealed."

He began to long for another draught of the warm, sulphurous water. But the faint hope they both entertained, that the dog might be leading them to some camping spot of hunter or Indian, made them afraid to turn back.

It was past the middle of the day when Wilfred perceived a round dark spot rising out of the snow, towards which the dog was hurrying. The snow beat full in their faces, but with the eddying gusts which almost swept them off their feet the Cree's keen sense of smell detected a whiff of smoke. This urged him on. Another and a surer sign of help at hand— the dog had vanished. Yet Maxica was sure he could hear him barking wildly in the distance. But Wilfred could no longer distinguish the round dark spot towards which they had been hastening. Maxica stood still in calm and proud despair. It was as impossible now to go, back to the *cache* of game and the sulphur spring as it was to force his way onward. They had reached a snow-drift. The soft yielding wall of white through which he was striding grew higher and higher.

In vain did Wilfred's eyes wander from one side to the other. As far as he could see the snow lay round them, one wide, white, level sheet, in which the Cree was standing elbow-deep. Were they, indeed, beyond the reach of human aid?

Wilfred was silent, hushed; but it was the hush of secret prayer.

Suddenly Maxica exclaimed, "Can the Good Spirit the white men talk of, can he hear us? Will he show us the path?"

Such a question from such wild lips, at such an hour, how strangely it struck on Wilfred's ear. He had scarcely voice enough left to make himself heard, for the storm was raging round them more fiercely than ever.

"I was thinking of him, Maxica. While we are yet speaking, will he hear?"

Wilfred's words were cut short, for Maxica had caught his foot against something buried in the snow, and stumbled. Wilfred was thrown forward. The ground seemed giving way beneath him. He was tumbled through the roof of the little birch-bark hut, which they had been wandering round and round without knowing it. Wilfred was only aware of a faint glimmer of light through a column of curling, blinding smoke. He thought he must be descending a chimney, but his outstretched hands were already touching the ground, and he wondered more and more where he could have alighted. Not so Maxica. He had grasped the firm pole supporting the fragile birch-bark walls, through which Wilfred had forced his way. One touch was sufficient to convince him they had groped their way to an Indian hut. The column of smoke rushing through the hole Wilfred had made in his most lucky tumble told the Cree of warmth and shelter within.

There was a scream from a feeble woman's voice, but the exclamation was in the rich, musical dialect of the Blackfeet, the hereditary enemies of his tribe. In the blind warrior's mind it was a better thing to hide himself beneath the snow and freeze to death, than submit to the scalping-knife of a hated foe.

Out popped Wilfred's head to assure him there was only a poor old woman inside, but she had got a fire.

The latter half of his confidences had been already made plain by the dense smoke, which was producing such a state of strangulation Wilfred could say no more.

But the hut was clearing; Maxica once more grasped the nearest pole, and swung himself down.

A few words with the terrified squaw were enough for the Cree, who knew so well the habits of their wandering race. The poor old creature had probably journeyed many hundreds of miles, roaming over their wide hunting-grounds, until she had sunk by the way, too exhausted to proceed any further. Then her people had built her this little hut, lit a fire in the hastily-piled circle of stones in the middle of it, heaped up the dry wood on one side to feed it, placed food and water on the other, and left her lying on her blankets to die alone. It was the custom of the wild, wandering tribes. She had accepted her fate with Indian resignation, simply saying that her hour had come. But the rest she so much needed had restored her failing powers, and whilst her stock of food lasted she was getting better. They had found her gathering together the last handful of sticks to make up the fire once more, and then she would lie down before it and starve. Every Indian knows what starvation means, and few can bear it as well. Living as they do entirely by the chase, the feast which follows the successful hunt is too often succeeded by a lengthy fast. Her shaking hands were gathering up the lumps of snow which had come down on the pieces of the broken roof, to fill her empty kettle.

Wilfred picked up the bits of bark to which it had been sticking, and threw them on the fire.

"My bow and quiver for a few old shreds of beaver-skin, and we are saved," groaned the Cree, who knew that all his garments were made from the deer. He felt the hem of the old squaw's tattered robe, but beaver there was none.

"What do you want it for, Maxica?" asked Wilfred, as he pulled off his gloves and offered them to him. "There is nothing about me that I would not give you, and be only too delighted to have got it to give, when I think how you carried me through the snowdrift. These are new beaver-skin;

31

take them, Maxica."

A smile lit up the chief's dark face as he carefully felt the proffered gloves, and to make assurance doubly sure added taste to touch. Then he began to tear them into shreds, which he directed Wilfred to drop into the melting snow in the kettle, explaining to him as well as he could that there was an oiliness in the beaver-skin which never quite dried out of it, and would boil down into a sort of soup.

"A kind of coarse isinglass, I should say," put in Wilfred. But the Cree knew nothing of isinglass and its nourishing qualities; yet he knew the good of the beaver-skin when other food had failed. It was a wonderful discovery to Wilfred, to think his gloves could provide them all with a dinner; but they required some long hours' boiling, and the fire was dying down again for want of fuel. Maxica ventured out to search for driftwood under the snow. He carefully drew out a pole from the structure of the hut, and using it as an alpenstock, swung himself out of the hollow in which the hut had been built for shelter, and where the snow had accumulated to such a depth that it was completely buried.

Whilst he was gone Wilfred and the squaw were beside the fire, sitting on the ground face to face, regarding each other attentively.

CHAPTER V.

IN THE BIRCH-BARK HUT.

The squaw was a very ugly woman; starvation and old age combined had made her perfectly hideous. As Wilfred sat in silence watching the simmering kettle, he thought she was the ugliest creature he had ever seen. Her complexion was a dark red-brown. Her glittering black eyes seemed to glare on him in the darkness of the hut like a cat's. Her shrivelled lips showed a row of formidably long teeth, which made Wilfred think of Little Red Ridinghood's grandmother, and he hoped she would not pounce on him and devour him before Maxica returned.

He wronged her shamefully, for she had been watching his limping movements with genuine pity. What did it matter that her gown was scant and short, or that her leggings, which had once been of bright-coloured cloth, curiously worked with beads, were reduced by time to a sort of no-colour and the tracery upon them to a dirty line? They hid a good, kind heart.

She loosened the English handkerchief tied over her head, and the long,

32

raven locks, now streaked with white, fell over her shoulders.

She was a wild-looking being, but her awakening glance of alertness need not have alarmed Wilfred, for she was only intent upon dipping him a cup of water from the steaming kettle. She was careful to taste it and cool it with a little of the snow still driving through the hole in the roof, until she made it the right degree of heat that was safest for Wilfred in his starving, freezing condition.

"What would Aunt Miriam think if she could see me now?" mused the boy, as he fixed his eyes on the dying embers and turned away from the steaming cup he longed to snatch at.

Yet when the squaw held it towards him, he put it back with a smile, resolutely repeating "After you," for was she not a woman?

He made her drink. A little greasy water, oh! how nice! Then he refilled the cup and took his share.

The tottering creature smoothed the blanket from which she had risen on Wilfred's summary entrance, and motioned to him to lie down.

"It will be all glove with us now," laughed Wilfred to himself—"hand and glove with the Red Indians. If any one whispered that in uncle's ear, wouldn't he think me a queer fish! But I owe my life to Maxica, and I know it."

He threw himself down on the blanket, glad indeed of the rest for his swollen ankle. From this lowly bed he fell to contemplating his temporary refuge. It looked so very temporary, especially the side from which Maxica had abstracted his alpenstock, Wilfred began to fear the next disaster would be its downfall. He was dozing, when a sudden noise made him start up, in the full belief the catastrophe he had dreaded had arrived; but it was only Maxica dropping the firewood he had with difficulty collected through the hole in the roof.

He called out to Wilfred that he had discovered his atim digging in the snow at some distance.

What his atim might prove to be Wilfred could not imagine. He was choosing a stick from the heap of firewood. Balancing himself on one foot, he popped his head through the hole to reconnoitre. He fancied he too could see a moving speck in the distance.

"The dog!" he cried joyfully, giving a long, shrill whistle that brought it bounding over the crisping snow towards him with a ptarmigan in its

33

mouth.

After much coaxing, Wilfred induced the dog to lay the bird down, to lap the melting snow which was filling the hollows in the floor with little puddles.

The squaw pounced upon the bird as a welcome addition to the beaver-skin soup. Where had the dog found it? He had not killed it, that was clear, for it was frozen hard. Yet it had not been frozen to death. The quick Indian perception of the squaw pointed to the bite on its breast. It was not the tooth of a dog, but the sharp beak of some bird of prey which had killed it. The atim had found the *cache* of a great white owl; a provident bird, which, when once its hunger is satisfied, stores the remainder of its prey in some handy crevice.

The snow had ceased to fall. The moon was rising. The thick white carpet which covered all around was hardening under the touch of the coming frost.

Another cup from the half-made soup, and Maxica proposed to start with Wilfred to search for the supposed store. The dog was no longer hungry. It had stretched itself on the ground at Wilfred's feet for a comfortable slumber.

An Indian never stops for pain or illness. With the grasp of death upon him, he will follow the war-path or the hunting track, so that Maxica paid no regard to Wilfred's swollen foot. If the boy could not walk, his shoulder was ready, but go he must; the atim would lead his own master to the spot, but it would never show it to a stranger.

Wilfred glanced up quickly, and then looked down with a nod to himself. It would not do to make much of his hurt in such company. Well, he had added a word to his limited stock of Indian. "Atim" was Cree for dog, that at least was clear; and they had added the atim to his slender possessions. They thought the dog was his own, and why should not he adopt him? They were both lost, they might as well be chums.

This conclusion arrived at, Wilfred caught up the wing of the ptarmigan, and showing it to the dog did his best to incite him to find another. He caught sight of a long strip of moose-skin which had evidently tied up the squaw's blanket on her journey. He persuaded her to lend it to him, making more use of signs than of words.

"Ugh! ugh!" she replied, and her "yes" was as intelligible to Wilfred as

34

Diomé's "caween." He soon found that "yes" and "no" alone can go a good way in making our wants understood by any one as naturally quick and observant as an Indian.

The squaw saw what Wilfred was trying to do, and helped him, feeble as she was, to make a sling for his foot. With the stick in his hand, when this was accomplished, he managed to hobble after Maxica and the dog.

The Cree went first, treading down a path, and partially clearing the way before him with his pole. But a disappointment awaited them. The dog led them intelligently enough to the very spot where it had unquestionably found a most abundant dinner, by the bones and feathers still sticking in the snow. Maxica, guided by his long experience, felt about him until he found two rats, still wedged in a hole in a decaying tree which had gone down before the gale. But he would not take them, for fear the owl might abandon her reserve.

"The otowuck-oho," said Maxica, mimicking the cry of the formidable bird, "will fill it again before the dawn. Wait and watch. Maxica have the otowuck himself. See!"

With all the skill of the Indian at constructing traps, he began his work, intending to catch the feathered Nimrod by one leg the next time it visited its larder, when all in a moment an alarm was sounded—a cry that rent the air, so hoarse, so hollow, and so solemn Wilfred clung to his guide in the chill of fear. It was a call that might have roused to action a whole garrison of soldiers. The Indian drew back. Again that dread "Waugh O!" rang out, and then the breathless silence which followed was broken by half-suppressed screams, as of some one suffocating in the throttling grasp of an enemy.

The dog, with his tail between his legs, crouched cowering at their feet.

"The Blackfeet are upon us," whispered the Cree, with his hand on his bow, when a moving shadow became visible above the distant pine trees.

The Cree breathed freely, and drew aside his half-made trap, abandoned at the first word that broke from Wilfred's lips: "It is not human; it is coming through the air."

"It is the otowuck itself," answered Maxica. "Be off, or it will have our eyes out if it finds us near its roost."

He was looking round him for some place of concealment. On came the dreaded creature, sailing in rapid silence towards its favourite haunt, gliding with outstretched pinions over the glistening snow, its great round eyes flashing like stars, or gleams of angry lightning, as it swept the whitened earth, shooting downwards to strike at some furry prey, then rising as suddenly in the clear, calm night, until it floated like a fleecy cloud above their heads, as ready to swoop upon the sparrow nestling on its tiny twig as upon the wild turkey-hen roosting among the stunted bushes.

Maxica trembled for the dog, for he knew the special hatred with which it regarded dogs. If it recognized the thief at its hoard, its doom was sealed.

Maxica pushed his alpenstock into an empty badger hole big enough for the boy and dog to creep into. Then, as the owl drew near, he sent an arrow whizzing through the air. It was aimed at the big white breast, but the unerring precision of other days was over. It struck the feathery wing. The bird soared aloft unharmed, and the archer, crouching in the snow, barely escaped its vengeance. Down it pounced, striking its talons in his shoulder, as he turned his back towards it to protect his face. Wilfred sprang out of the friendly burrow, snatched the pole from Maxica's hand, and beat off the owl; and the dog, unable to rush past Wilfred, barked furiously. The onslaught and the noise were at least distasteful. Hissing fiercely, with the horn-like feathers above its glaring eyes erect and bristling, the bird spread its gigantic wings, wheeling slowly and gracefully above their ambush; for Wilfred had retreated as quickly as he had emerged, and Maxica lay on his face as still as death. More attractive game presented itself. A hawk flew past. What hawk could resist the pleasure of a passing pounce? Away went the two, chasing and fighting, across the snowy waste.

Wilfred sprang and beat off the owl.

36

When the owl was out of sight, the Cree rose to his feet to complete the snare. Wilfred crept out of his burrow, to find his fingers as hard and white and useless as if they had turned to stone. He had kept his gloveless hands well cuddled up in the long sleeves of his coat during the walk, but their exposure to the cold when he struck at the owl had changed them to a lump of ice.

Maxica heard the exclamation, "Oh, my hands! my hands!" and seizing a great lump of snow began to rub them vigorously.

The return to the hut was easier than the outgoing, for the snow was harder. The pain in Wilfred's fingers was turning him sick and faint as they reached the hut a little past midnight.

The gloves were reduced to jelly, but the state of Wilfred's hands troubled the old squaw. She had had her supper from the beaver-skin soup, but was quite ready, Indian fashion, to begin again.

The three seated themselves on the floor, and the cup was passed from one to the other, until the whole of the soup was drank.

The walk had been fruitless, as Wilfred said. They had returned with nothing but the key of the big owl's larder, which, after such an encounter, it would probably desert.

The Cree lit his pipe, the squaw lay down to sleep, and Wilfred talked to his dog.

"Do you understand our bargain, old fellow?" he asked. "You and I are going to chum together. Now it is clear I must give you a name. Let us see which you will like best."

Wilfred ran through a somewhat lengthy list, for nowhere but in Canada are dogs accommodated with such an endless variety. There are names in constant use from every Indian dialect, but of the Atims and the Chistlis the big, old fellow took no heed. He sat up before his new master, looking very sagacious, as if he quite entered into the important business of choosing a name. But clearly Indian would not do. even Mist-atim, which Wilfred could now interpret as "big dog,"—a name the Cree usually bestows upon his horse,—was heard with a contemptuous "Ach!" Chistli, "seven dogs" in the Sircie dialect, which appeared to Wilfred highly complimentary to his furry friend, met with no recognition. Then he went over the Spankers and Ponys and Boxers, to which the numerous hauling dogs so often responded. No better success. The pricked ears were more erect than ever. The head was turned away in positive indifference.

"Are you a Frenchman?" asked Wilfred, going over all the old French names he could remember. Diomé thought the dogs had a special partiality for French. It would not do, however. This particular dog might hate it. There were Yankee names in plenty from over the border, and uncouth sounding Esquimau from the far north.

Wilfred began to question if his dog had ever had a name, when Yula caught his ear, and "Yula chummie" brought the big shaggy head rubbing on Wilfred's knee. Few dogs are honoured with the choice of their own name, but it answered, and "Yula chummie" was adhered to by boy and dog.

This weighty matter settled, Wilfred was startled to see Maxica rouse himself up with a shake, and look to the man-hole, as the Cree called their place of exit. He was going. Wilfred sprang up in alarm.

"Don't leave me!" he entreated. "How shall I ever find my way home without you?"

It might be four o'clock, for the east was not yet gray, and the morning stars shone brightly on the glistening snow. Maxica paused, regarding earth and sky attentively, until he had ascertained the way of the wind. It was still blowing from the north-east. More snow was surely coming. His care was for his canoe, which he had left in safe mooring by the river bank. No one but an Indian could have hoped, in his forlorn condition, to have recovered the lost path to the running stream. His one idea was to grope about until he did find it, with the wonderful persistency of his race. The Indian rarely fails in anything he sets his mind to accomplish. But to take the lame boy with him was out of the question. He might have many miles to traverse before he reached the spot. He tried to explain to Wilfred that he must now pack up his canoe for the winter. He was going to turn it keel upwards, among the branches of some strong tree, and cover it with boughs, until the spring of the leaf came round again.

"Will it be safe?" asked Wilfred.

"Safe! perfectly."

Maxica's own particular mark was on boat and paddle. No Indian, no hunter would touch it. Who else was there in that wide, lone land? As for Wilfred, his own people would come and look for him, now the storm was over.

"I am not so sure of that," said the poor boy sadly, remembering Bowkett's words.—"My aunt Miriam did not take to me. She may not trouble herself about me. How could I be so stupid as to set her against me," he was thinking, "all for nothing?"

"Then," urged Maxica, "stay here with the Far-off-Dawn"—for that was the old squaw's name. In his Indian tongue he called her Pe-na-Koam. "Will not the Good Spirit take care of you? Did not he guide us out of the snowdrift?"

Wilfred was silenced. "I never did think much of myself," he said at last, "but I believe I grow worse and worse. How is it that I know and don't know—that I cannot realize this love that never will forsake; always more ready to hear than we to ask? If I could but feel it true, all true for me, I should not be afraid."

Under that longing the trust was growing stronger and stronger in his heart.

"I shall come again for the moose," said Maxica, as he shook the red and aching fingers which just peeped out from Wilfred's long sleeve; and so he left him.

The boy watched the Indian's lithe figure striding across the snow, until he could see him no longer. Then a cold, dreary feeling crept over him. Was he abandoned by all the world—forgotten—disliked? Did nobody care for him? He tucked his hands into the warm fur which folded over his breast, and tried to throw off the fear. The tears gushed from his eyes. Well, there was nobody to see.

He had forgotten Yula. Those unwonted raindrops had brought him, wondering and troubled, to Wilfred's side. A big head was poking its way under his arm, and two strong paws were brushing at his knee. Yula was saying, "Don't, don't cry," in every variety of doggie language. Never had he been so loving, so comforting, so warm to hug, so quick to understand. He was doing his best to melt the heavy heart's lead that was weighing poor Wilfred down.

He built up the fire, and knelt before it, with Yula's head on his shoulder; for the cold grew sharper in the gray of the dawn. The squaw, now the pangs of hunger were so far appeased, was sleeping heavily. But there was no sleep for Wilfred. As the daylight grew stronger he went again to his look-out. His thoughts were turning to Forgill. He had seen so much more of Forgill than of any one else at his uncle's, and he had been so careful over him on the journey. It was wrong to think they would all forget him. He would trust and hope.

He filled the kettle with fresh snow, and put it on to boil.

The sun was streaming through the hole in the roof when the squaw awoke, like another creature, but not in the least surprised to find Maxica had departed. She seemed thankful to see the fire still burning, and poured out her gratitude to Wilfred. Her smiles and gestures gave the meaning of the words he did not understand.

Then he asked himself, "What would have become of her if he too had gone away with Maxica?"

She looked pityingly at Wilfred's unfortunate fingers as he offered her a cup of hot water, their sole breakfast. But they could not live on hot water. Where was the daily bread to come from for them both? Pe-na-Koam was making signs. Could Wilfred set a trap? Alas! he knew nothing of the Indian traps and snares. He sent out Yula to forage for himself, hoping he might bring them back a bird, as he had done the night before. Wilfred lingered by the hole in the roof, watching him dashing through the snow, and casting many a wistful glance to the far-away south, almost expecting to see Forgill's fur cap and broad capote advancing towards him; for help would surely come. But there are the slow, still hours, as well as the sudden bursts of storm and sunshine. All have their share in the making of a brave and constant spirit. God's time is not our time, as Wilfred had yet to learn.

CHAPTER VI.

SEARCHING FOR A SUPPER.

Pe-na-Koam insisted upon examining Wilfred's hands and feet, and tending to them after her native fashion. She would not suffer him to leave the hut, but ventured out herself, for the storm was followed by a day of glorious sunshine. She returned with her lap full of a peculiar kind of moss, which she had scraped from under the snow. In her hand she carried a bunch of fine brown fibres.

"Wattape!" she exclaimed, holding them up before him, with such evident pleasure he thought it was something to eat; but no, the moss went into the kettle to boil for dinner, but the wattape was laid carefully aside.

The squaw had been used to toil from morning to night, doing all the work of her little world, whilst her warrior, when under shelter, slept or smoked by the fire. She expected no help from Wilfred within the hut, but she wanted to incite him to go and hunt. She took a sharp-pointed stick and drew a bow and arrow on the floor. Then she made sundry figures. which he took for traps; but he could only shake his head. He was thinking of a visit to the owl's tree. But when they had eaten the moss, Pe-na-Koam drew out a piece of skin from under her blanket, and spreading it on the floor laid her fingers beseechingly on his hunting-knife. With this she cut him out a pair of gloves, fingerless it is true, shaped like a baby's first glove, but oh! so warm. Wilfred now discovered the use of the wattape, as she drew out one long thread after another, and began to sew the gloves together with it, pricking the holes through which she passed it with a quill she produced from some part of her dress.

Wilfred took up the brown tangle and examined it closely. It had been torn from the fine fibrous root of the pine. He stood still to watch her, wondering whether there was anything he could do. He took the stick she had used and drew the rough figure of a man fishing on the earthen floor. He felt sure they must be near some stream or lakelet. The Indians would never have left her beyond the reach of water. The wrinkled face lit up with hopeful smiles. Away she worked more diligently than ever.

Wilfred built up the fire to give her a better blaze. They had wood enough to last them through to-morrow. Before it was all burnt up he must try to get in some more. The use was returning to his hands. He took up some of the soft mud, made by the melting of the snow on the earthen floor, and tried to stop up the cracks in the bark which formed the walls of the hut.

They both worked on in silence, hour after hour, as if there were not a moment to lose. At last the gloves were finished. The Far-off-Dawn considered her blanket, and decided a piece might be spared off every corner. Out of these she cut a pair of socks. The Indians themselves often wear three or four pairs of such blanket socks at once in the very coldest of the weather. But Wilfred could find nothing in the hut out of which to make a fishing line. The only thing he could do was to pay a visit to the white owl's larder. He was afraid to touch Maxica's trap. He did not think he could manage it. Poor boy, his spirit was failing him for want of food. Yet he determined to go and see if there was anything to be found. Wilfred got up with an air of resolution, and began to arrange the sling for his foot. But the Far-off-Dawn soon made him understand he must not go without his socks, which she was hurrying to finish.

"I believe I am changing into a snail," thought Wilfred; "I do nothing but crawl about. Yet twenty slips brought the snail to the top of his wall. Twenty slips and twenty climbs—that is something to think of."

The moon was rising. The owl would leave her haunt to seek for prey.

"Now it strikes me," exclaimed Wilfred, "why she always perches on a leafless tree. Her blinking eyes are dazzled by the flicker of the leaves: but they are nearly gone now, she will have a good choice. She may not go far a-field, if she does forsake her last night's roost." This reflection was wondrously consolatory.

The squaw had kept her kettle filled with melting snow all day, so that they could both have a cup of hot water whenever they liked. The Far-off-Dawn was as anxious to equip him for his foraging expedition as he was to take it. The socks were finished; she had worked hard, and Wilfred knew it. He began to think there was something encouraging in her very name— the Far-off-Dawn. Was it not what they were waiting for? It was an earnest that their night would end.

She made him put both the blanket socks on the swollen foot, and then persuaded him to exchange his boots for her moccasins, which were a much better protection against the snow. The strip of fur, no longer needed to protect his toes, was wound round and round his wrists.

Then the squaw folded her blanket over his shoulder, and started him, pointing out as well as she could the streamlet and the pool which had supplied her with water when she was strong enough to fetch it.

Both knew their lives depended upon his success. Yula was by his side. Wilfred turned back with a great piece of bark, to cover up the hole in the roof of the hut to keep the squaw warm. She had wrapped the skin over her feet and was lying before the fire, trying to sleep in her dumb despair. She had discovered there was no line and hook forthcoming from any one of his many pockets. How then could he catch the fish with which she knew the Canadian waters everywhere abounded?

Pe-na-Koam had pointed out the place of the pool so earnestly that Wilfred thought, "I will go there first; perhaps it was there she found the moss."

The northern lights were flashing overhead, shooting long lines of roseate glory towards the zenith, as if some unseen angel's hand were stringing heaven's own harp. But the full chord which flowed beneath its touch was light instead of music.

Wilfred stood silent, rapt in admiring wonder, as he gazed upon those glowing splendours, forgetting everything beside. Yula recalled him to the work in hand. He hobbled on as fast as he could. He was drawing near the pool, for tall rushes bent and shivered above the all-covering snow, and pines and willows rocked in the night wind overhead. Another wary step, and the pool lay stretched before him like a silver shield.

A colony of beavers had made their home in this quiet spot, building their mounds of earth like a dam across the water. But the busy workers were all settling within doors to their winter sleep—drawbridges drawn up, and gates barred against intruders. "You are wiseheads," thought Wilfred, "and I almost wish I could do the same—work all summer like bees, and sleep all winter like dormice; but then the winter is so long."

"Would not it be a grand thing to take home a beaver, Yula?" he exclaimed, suddenly remembering his gloves in their late reduced condition, and longing for another cup of the unpalatable soup; for the keen air sharpened the keener appetite, until he felt as if he could have eaten the said gloves, boiled or unboiled.

But how to get at the clever sleepers under their well-built dome was the difficulty, almost the impossibility.

"Yula, it can't be done—that is by you and me, old boy," he sighed. "We have not got their house-door key for certain. We shall have to put up with the moss, and think ourselves lucky if we find it."

The edge of the pool was already fringed with ice, and many a shallow basin where it had overflowed its banks was already frozen over. Wilfred was brushing away the crisp snow in his search for moss, when he caught sight of a big white fish, made prisoner by the ice in an awkward corner, where the rising flood had one day scooped a tiny reservoir. Making Yula sit down in peace and quietness, and remember manners, he set to work. He soon broke the ice with a blow from the handle of his knife, and took out the fish. As he expected, the hungry dog stood ready to devour it; but Wilfred, suspecting his intention, tied it up in the blanket, and swung it over his shoulder. Fortune did not favour him with such another find, although he searched about the edge of the lake until it grew so slippery he was afraid of falling in. He had now to retrace his steps, following the marks in the snow back to the hut.

The joy of Pe-na-Koam was unbounded when he untied the blanket and slid the fish into her hands.

The prospect of the hot supper it would provide for them nerved Wilfred to go a little further and try to reach the big owl's roost, for fear another snow should bury the path Maxica had made to it. Once lost he might never find it again. The owl was still their most trusty friend and most formidable foe. Thanks to the kindly labours of Maxica's pole, Wilfred could trudge along much faster now; but before he reached the hollow tree, strange noises broke the all-pervading stillness. There was a barking of dogs in the distance, to which Yula replied with all the energy in his nature. There was a tramping as of many feet, and of horses, coming nearer and nearer with a lumbering thud on the ground, deadened and muffled by the snow, but far too plain not to attract all Wilfred's attention.

There was a confusion of sounds, as of a concourse of people; too many for a party of hunters, unless the winter camp of which Diomé had spoken was assembling. Oh joy! if this could be. Wilfred was working himself into a state of excitement scarcely less than Yula's.

He hurried on to the roosting-tree, for it carried him nearer still to the trampling and the hum.

What could it mean? Yula was before him, paws up, climbing the old dead trunk, bent still lower by the recent storm. A snatch, and he had something out of that hole in the riven bark. Wilfred scrambled on, for fear his dog should forestall him. The night was clear around him, he saw the aurora flashes come and go. Yula had lain down at the foot of the tree, devouring his prize. Wilfred's hand, fumbling in its fingerless gloves, at last found the welcome hole. It was full once more. Soft feathers and furs: a gopher—the small ground squirrel—crammed against some little snow-birds.

Wilfred gave the squirrel to his dog, for he had many fears the squaw would be unwilling to give him anything but water in their dearth of food. The snow-birds he transferred to his pocket, looking nervously round as he did so; but there was no owl in sight. The white breasts of the snow-birds were round and plump; but they were little things, not much bigger than sparrows, and remembering Maxica's caution, he dare not take them all.

His hand went lower: a few mice—he could leave them behind him without any reluctance. But stop, he had not got to the bottom yet. Better than ever: he had felt the webbed feet of a wild duck. Mrs. Owl was nearly

44

forgiven the awful scare of the preceding night. Growing bolder in his elation, Wilfred seated himself on the roots of the tree, from which Yula's ascent had cleared the snow. He began to prepare his game, putting back the skin and feathers to conceal his depredations from the savage tenant, lest she should change her domicile altogether.

"I hope she can't count," said Wilfred, who knew not how to leave the spot without ascertaining the cause of the sounds, which kept him vibrating between hope and fear.

Suddenly Yula sprang forward with a bound and rushed over the snow-covered waste with frantic fury.

"The Blackfeet! the Blackfeet!" gasped Wilfred, dropping like lightning into the badger hole where Maxica had hidden him from the owl's vengeance. A singular cavalcade came in sight: forty or fifty Indian warriors, armed with their bows and guns and scalping-knives, the chiefs with their eagles' feathers nodding as they marched. Behind them trotted a still greater number of ponies, on which their squaws were riding man fashion, each with her pappoose or baby tucked up as warm as it could be in its deer-skin, and strapped safely to its wooden cradle, which its mother carried on her back.

Every pony was dragging after it what the Indians call a travoy—that is, two fir poles, the thin ends of which are harnessed to the pony's shoulders, while the butt ends drag on the ground; another piece of wood is fastened across them, making a sort of truck, on which the skins and household goods are piled. The bigger children were seated on the top of many a well-laden travoy, so that the squaws came on but slowly.

Wilfred was right in his conjecture: they were the Blackfeet Maxica feared to encounter, coming up to trade with the nearest Hudson Bay Company's fort. They were bringing piles of furs and robes of skin, and bags of pemmican, to exchange for shot and blankets, sugar and tea, beads, and such other things as Indians desire to possess. They always came up in large parties, because they were crossing the hunting-grounds of their enemies the Crees. They had a numerous following of dogs, and many a family of squalling puppies, on the children's laps.

The grave, stern, savage aspect of the men, the ugly, anxious, careworn faces of the toiling women, filled Wilfred with alarm. Maxica in his semi-blindness might well fear to be the one against so many. Wilfred dared not even call back Yula, for fear of attracting their attention. They were passing on to encamp by the pool he had just quitted. Friendly or unfriendly, Yula was barking and snarling in the midst of the new-comers.

"Was his Yula, his Yula chummie, going to leave him?" asked Wilfred in his dismay. "What if he had belonged originally to this roving tribe, and they should take him away!" This thought cut deeper into Wilfred's heart than anything else at that moment. He crept out of his badger hole, and crawled along the ditch-like path, afraid to show his head above the snow, and still more afraid to remain where he was, for fear of the owl's return.

He kept up a hope that Yula might come back of his own accord. He was soon at the birch-bark hut, but no Yula had turned up.

He tumbled in, breathless and panting. Pe-na-Koam was sure he had been frightened, but thought only of the owl. She had run a stick through the tail of the fish, and was broiling it in the front of the fire. The cheery light flickered and danced along the misshapen walls, which seemed to lean more and more each day from the pressure of the snow outside them.

"The blessed snow!" exclaimed Wilfred. "It hides us so completely no one can see there is a hut at all, unless the smoke betrays us."

How was he to make the squaw understand the dreaded Blackfeet were here? He snatched up their drawing stick, as he called it, and began to sketch in a rough and rapid fashion the moving Indian camp which he had seen. A man with a bow in his hand, with a succession of strokes behind him to denote his following, and a horse's head with the poles of the travoy, were quite sufficient to enlighten the aged woman. She grasped Wilfred's hand and shook it. Then she raised her other arm, as if to strike, and looked inquiringly in his face. Friend or foe? That was the all-important question neither could answer.

Before he returned his moccasins to their rightful owner, Wilfred limped out of the hut and hung up the contents of his blanket game-bag in the nearest pine. They were already frozen.

Not knowing what might happen if their refuge were discovered, they seated themselves before the fire to enjoy the supper Wilfred had secured. The fish was nearly the size of a salmon trout. The squaw removed the sticks from which it depended a little further from the scorch of the fire, and fell to—pulling off the fish in flakes from one side of the backbone, and signing to Wilfred to help himself in similar fashion from the other.

"Fingers were made before forks," thought the boy, his hunger overcoming all reluctance to satisfy it in such a heathenish way. But the old squaw's brow was clouded and her thoughts were troubled. She was trembling for Wilfred's safety.

She knew by the number of dashes on the floor the party was large—a band of her own people; no other tribe journeyed as they did, moving the whole camp at once. Other camps dispersed, not more than a dozen families keeping together.

If they took the boy for a Cree or the friend of a Cree, they would count him an enemy. Before the fish had vanished her plan was made.

She brought Wilfred his boots, and took back her moccasins. As the boy pulled off the soft skin sock, which drew to the shape of his foot without any pressure that could hurt his sprain, feeling far more like a glove than a shoe, he wondered at the skill which had made it. He held it to the fire to examine the beautiful silk embroidery on the legging attached to it. His respect for his companion was considerably increased. It was difficult to believe that beads and dyed porcupine quills and bright-coloured skeins of silk had been the delight of her life. But just now she was intent upon getting possession of his hunting-knife. With this she began to cut up the firewood into chips and shavings. Wilfred thought he should be the best at that sort of work, and went to her help, not knowing what she intended to do with it.

In her nervous haste she seemed at first glad of his assistance. Then she pulled the wood out of his hand, stuck the knife in his belt, and implored him by gestures to sit down in a hole in the floor close against the wall, talking to him rapidly in her soft Indian tongue, as if she were entreating him to be patient.

Wilfred thought this was a queer kind of game, which he did not half like, and had a good mind to turn crusty. But the tears came into her aged eyes. She clasped her hands imploringly, kissed him on both cheeks, as if to assure him of her good intentions, looked to the door, and laid a finger on his lips impressively. In the midst of this pantomime it struck Wilfred suddenly "she wants to hide me." Soon the billet stack was built over him with careful skill, and the chips and shavings flung on the top.

CHAPTER VII.

FOLLOWING THE BLACKFEET.

There was many a little loophole in Wilfred's hiding-place through which he could take a peep unseen. The squaw had let the fire die down to a smouldering heap, and this she had carefully covered over with bark, so that there was neither spark nor flame to shine through the broken roof. The hut was unusually clear of smoke, and all was still.

Wilfred was soon nodding dangerously behind his billet-stack, forgetting in his drowsy musings the instability of his surroundings. The squaw rose up from the floor, and replaced the knot of wood he had sent rolling. He dreamed of Yula's bark in the distance, and wakened to find the noise a reality, but not the bark. It was not his Yula wanting to be let in, as he imagined, but a confused medley of sounds suggestive of the putting up of tent poles. There was the ring of the hatchet among the trees, the crash of the breaking boughs, the thud of the falling trunk. Even Wilfred could not entertain a doubt that the Blackfeet were encamping for the night alarmingly near their buried hut. In silence and darkness was their only safeguard. It was all for the best Yula had run away, his uneasy growls would have betrayed them.

Midnight came and passed; the sounds of work had ceased, but the galloping of the ponies, released from the travoys, the scraping of their hoofs seeking a supper beneath the snow, kept Wilfred on the rack. The echo of the ponies' feet seemed at times so near he quite expected to see a horse's head looking down through the hole, or, worse still, some unwary kick might demolish their fragile roof altogether.

With the gray of the dawn the snow began again to fall. Was ever snow more welcome? The heavy flakes beat back the feeble column of smoke, and hissed on the smouldering wood, as they found ready entrance through the parting in the bark which did duty for a chimney. No matter, it was filling up the path which Maxica had made and obliterating every footprint around the hut. It seemed to Wilfred that the great feathery flakes were covering all above them, like a sheltering wing.

The tell-tale duck, the little snow-birds he had hung on the pine branch would all be hidden now. Not a chink was left in the bark through which the gray snow-light of the wintry morning could penetrate.

In spite of their anxiety, both the anxious watchers had fallen asleep. The squaw was the first to rouse. Wilfred's temporary trap-door refused to move when, finding all was still around them, she had tried to push it aside; for the hut was stifling, and she wanted snow to refill the kettle.

The fire was out, and the snow which had extinguished it was already stiffening. She took a half-burnt brand from the hearth, and, mounting the stones which surrounded the fireplace, opened the smoke-vent; for there the snow had not had time to harden, although the frost was setting in with the daylight. To get out of their hut in another hour might be impossible. With last night's supper, a spark of her former energy had returned. A piece of the smoke-dried bark gave way and precipitated an avalanche of snow into the tiny hut.

Wilfred wakened with a start. The daylight was streaming down upon him, and the squaw was gone. What could have happened while he slept? How he blamed himself for going to sleep at all. But then he could not live without it. As he wondered and waited and reasoned with himself thus, there was still the faint hope the squaw might return. Anyhow, Wilfred thought it was the wisest thing he could do to remain concealed where she had left him. If the Indians camping by the pool were her own people, they might befriend him too. Possibly she had gone over to their camp to ask for aid.

How long he waited he could not tell—it seemed an age—when he heard the joyful sound of Yula's bark. Down leaped the dog into the very midst of the fireplace, scattering the ashes, and bringing with him another avalanche of snow. But his exuberant joy was turned to desperation when he could not find his Wilfred. He was rushing round and round, scenting the ground where Wilfred had sat. Up went his head high in the air, as he gave vent to his feelings in a perfect yowl of despair.

"Yula! Yula!" called Wilfred softly. The dog turned round and tore at the billet-stack. Wilfred's defence was levelled in a moment; the wood went rolling in every direction, and Yula mounted the breach in triumph, digging out his master from the debris as a dog might dig out a fox. He would have him out, he would not give up. He tugged at Wilfred's arms, he butted his head under his knees; there was no resisting his impetuosity, he made him stand upright. When, as Yula evidently believed, he had set his master free, he bounded round him in an ecstasy of delight.

"You've done it, old boy," said Wilfred. "You've got me out of hiding; and neither you nor I can pile the wood over me again, so now, whatever

49

comes, we must face it together."

He clasped his arms round the thick tangle of hair that almost hid the two bright eyes, so full of love, that were gazing at him.

Wilfred could not help kissing the dear old blunderer, as he called him. "And now, Yula," he went on, "since you will have it so, we'll look about us."

Wilfred's foot was a good deal better. He could put his boot on for the first time. He mounted the stones which the squaw had piled, and listened. Yes, there were voices and laughter mingling with the neighing of the ponies and the lumbering sounds of the travoys. The camp was moving on. The "Far-off-Dawn" was further off than ever from him. He had no longer a doubt the squaw had gone with her people.

She had left him her kettle and the piece of skin. To an Indian woman her blanket is hood and cloak and muff all in one. She never goes out of doors without it.

Wilfred smoothed the gloves she had made him and pulled up the blanket socks. Oh, she had been good to him! He thought he understood it all now—that farewell kiss, and the desire to hide him until the fierce warriors of her tribe had passed on. He wrapped the skin over his shoulders, slung the kettle on his arm, chose out a good strong staff to lean on, and held himself ready for the chapter of accidents, whatever they might be.

No one came near him. The sounds grew fainter and fainter. The silence, the awful stillness, was creeping all around him once again. It became unbearable—the dread, the disappointment, the suspense. Wilfred climbed out of the hut and swung himself into the branches of the nearest pine. The duck and the snow-birds were frozen as hard as stones. But the fire was out long ago. Wilfred had no matches, no means of lighting it up again. He put back the game; even Yula could not eat it in that state. He swung himself higher up in the tree, just in time to catch sight of the vanishing train, winding its way along the vast snow-covered waste. He watched it fading to a moving line. What was it leaving behind? A lost boy. If Wilfred passed the night in the tree he would be frozen to death. If he crept back into the tumble-down hut he might be buried beneath another snow. If he went down to the pool he might find the ashes of the Indians' camp-fires still glowing. If they had left a fire behind them he must see the smoke—the snow-soaked branches were sure to smoke. The sleet was driving in his face, but he looked in vain for the dusky curling wreath that must have been visible at so short a distance.

Was all hope gone? His head grew dizzy. There were no words on his lips, and the bitter cry in his heart died mute. Then he seemed to hear again his mother's voice reading to him, as she used to read in far-off days by the evening fire: "I will not fail thee, nor forsake thee. Be strong, and of a good courage. Be not afraid, neither be thou dismayed. For the Lord thy God is with thee, whithersoever thou goest."

The Indian train was out of sight, but the trampling of those fifty ponies, dragging the heavily-laden travoys, had left a beaten track—a path so broad he could not lose it—and he knew that it would bring him to some white man's home.

Wilfred sprang down from the tree, decided, resolute. Better to try and find this shop in the wilderness than linger there and die. The snow beneath the tree was crisp and hard. Yula bounded on before him, eager to follow where the Blackfeet dogs had passed. They were soon upon the road, trudging steadily onward.

The dog had evidently shared the strangers' breakfast; he was neither hungry nor thirsty. Not so his poor little master, who was feeling very faint for want of a dinner, when he saw a bit of pemmican on the ground, dropped no doubt by one of the Indian children.

Wilfred snatched it up and began to eat. Pemmican is the Indians' favourite food. It is made of meat cut in slices and dried. It is then pounded between two smooth stones, and put in a bag of buffalo-skin. Melted fat is poured over it, to make it keep. To the best kinds of pemmican berries and sugar are added. It forms the most solid food a man can have. There are different ways of cooking it, but travellers, or voyageurs, as they are usually called in Canada, eat it raw. It was a piece of raw pemmican Wilfred had picked up. Hunger lent it the flavour it might have lacked at any other time.

With this for a late dinner, and a rest on a fallen tree, he felt himself once more, and started off again with renewed vigour. The sleet was increasing with the coming dusk. On he toiled, growing whiter and whiter, until his snow-covered figure was scarcely distinguishable from the frozen ground. Yula was powdered from head to foot; moreover, poor dog, he was obliged to stop every now and then to bite off the little icicles which were forming between his toes.

Fortunately for the weary travellers the sky began to clear when the moon arose. Before them stood dark ranks of solemn, stately pines, with here and there a poplar thicket rising black and bare from the sparkling ground. Their charred and shrivelled branches showed the work of the recent prairie fires, which had only been extinguished by the snowstorm.

Wilfred whistled Yula closer and closer to his side, as the forest echoes wakened to the moose-call and the wolf-howl. On, on they walked through the dusky shadows cast by the giant pines, until the strange meteors of the north lit up the icy night, flitting across the starry sky in such swift succession the Indians call it the dance of the dead spirits.

In a scene so weird and wild the boldest heart might quail. Wilfred felt his courage dwindling with every step, when Yula sprang forward with a bark that roused a sleeping herd, and Wilfred found himself in the midst of the Indian ponies, snorting and kicking at the disturber of their peace. The difficulty of getting Yula out again, without losing the track or rousing the camp, which they must now be approaching, engrossed Wilfred, and taxed his powers to their uttermost. He could see the gleam of their many watch-fires, and guided his course more warily. Imposing silence on Yula by every device he could imagine, he left the beaten track which would have taken him into the midst of the dreaded Blackfeet, and slanted further and further into the forest gloom, but not so far as to lose the glow of the Indians' fires. In the first faint gray of the wintry dawn he heard the rushing of a mighty fall, and found concealment in a wide expanse of frozen reeds and stunted willows.

Yula had been brought to order. A tired dog is far more manageable. He lay down at his master's feet, whilst Wilfred watched and listened. He was wide of the Blackfeet camp, yet not at such a distance as to be unable to distinguish the sounds of awakening life within it from the roar of the waterfall. To his right the ground was rising. He scarcely felt himself safe so near the Blackfeet, and determined to push on to the higher ground, where he would have a better chance of seeing what they were about. If they moved on, he could go back to their camping-place and gather the crumbs they might have let fall, and boil himself some water before their fires were extinguished, and then follow in their wake as before.

He began to climb the hill with difficulty, when he was aware of a thin, blue column of light smoke curling upwards in the morning air. It was not from the Indian camp. Had he nearly reached his goal? The light was steadily increasing, and he could clearly see on the height before him three or four tall pines, which had been stripped of their branches by the voyageur's axe, and left to mark a landing-place. These lop-sticks, as the Canadians call them, were a welcome sight. He reached them at last, and gained the view he had been longing to obtain. At his feet rolled the majestic river, plunging in one broad, white sheet over a hidden precipice.

In the still uncertain light of the early dawn the cataract seemed twice its actual size. The jagged tops of the pine trees on the other side of the river rose against the pale green of coming day. Close above the falls the bright star of the morning gleamed like a diamond on the rim of the descending flood; at its foot the silvery spray sprang high into the air, covering the gloomy pines which had reared their dark branches in many a crack and cleft with glittering spangles.

Nestling at the foot of the crag on which Wilfred stood was the well-built stockade of the trading-fort. The faint blue line of smoke which he had perceived was issuing from the chimney of the trader's house, but the inmates were not yet astir.

He brushed the tears from his eyes, but they were mingled tears of joy and thankfulness and exhaustion. As he was watching, a party of Indians stole out from their camp, and posted themselves among the frozen reeds which he had so recently vacated.

The chief, with a few of the Blackfeet, followed by three or four squaws laden with skins, advanced to the front of the stockade, where they halted. The chief was waving in his hand a little flag, to show that he had come to trade. After a while the sounds of life and movement began within the fort. The little group outside was steadily increasing in numbers. Some more of the Blackfeet warriors had loaded their horses and their wives, and were coming up behind their chief, with their heavy bags of pemmican hanging like panniers across the backs of the horses, whilst the poor women toiled after them with the piles of skins and leather.

All was bustle and activity inside the trader's walls. Wilfred guessed they were making all sorts of prudent preparations before they ventured to receive so large a party. He was thinking of the men in ambush among the reeds, and he longed to give some warning to the Hudson Bay officer, who could have no idea of the numbers lurking round his gate.

But how was this to be done in time? There was but one entrance to the fort. He was afraid to descend his hill and knock for admittance, under the lynx-like eyes of the Blackfoot chief, who was growing impatient, and was making fresh signs to attract the trader's attention.

53

At last there was a creaking sound from the fort. Bolts and bars were withdrawn, and the gate was slowly opened. Out came the Hudson Bay officer, carefully shutting it behind him. He was a tall, white-haired man, with an air of command about him, and the easy grace of a gentleman in every action. He surveyed his wild visitors for a moment or two, and then advanced to meet them with a smile of welcome. The chief came a step or two forward, shook hands with the white man, and began to make a speech. A few of his companions followed his example.

"Now," thought Wilfred, "while all this talking and speechifying is abroad, I may get a chance to reach the fort unobserved."

He slid down the steep hill, with Yula after him, crept along the back of the stockade, and round the end farthest from the reeds. In another moment he was at the gate. A gentle tap with his hand was all he dared to give. It met with no answer. He repeated it a little louder. Yula barked. The gate was opened just a crack, and a boy about his own age peeped out.

"Let me in," said Wilfred desperately. "I have something to tell you."

The crack was widened. Wilfred slipped in and Yula followed. The gate was shut and barred behind them.

"Well?" asked the boyish porter.

"There are dozens of Blackfeet Indians hiding among the frozen reeds. I saw them stealing down from their camp before it was light. I am afraid they mean mischief," said Wilfred, lowering his voice.

"We need to be careful," returned the other, glancing round at their many defences; "but who are you?"

"I belong to some settlers across the prairie. I have lost my way. I have been wandering about all night, following the trail of the Blackfeet. That is how I came to know and see what they were doing," replied Wilfred.

"They always come up in numbers," answered the stranger thoughtfully, "ready for a brush with the Crees. They seem friendly to us."

As the boy spoke he slipped aside a little shutter in the gate, and peeped through a tiny grill.

In the middle of the enclosure there was a wooden house painted white. Three or four iron funnels stuck out of the roof instead of chimneys, giving it a very odd appearance. There were a few more huts and sheds. But Wilfred's attention was called off from these surroundings, for a whole family of dogs had rushed out upon Yula, with a chorus of barking that deafened every other sound. For Yula had marched straight to the back door of the house, where food was to be had, and was shaking it and whining to be let in.

The young stranger Gaspé took a bit of paper and a pencil out of his pocket and wrote hastily: "There are lots more of the Blackfeet hiding amongst the reeds. What does that mean?"

"Louison!" he cried to a man at work in one of the sheds, "go outside and give this to grandfather."

CHAPTER VIII.

THE SHOP IN THE WILDERNESS.

As soon as Gaspé had despatched his messenger he turned to Wilfred, observing, in tones of grateful satisfaction, "I am so glad we know in time."

"Is that your grandfather?" asked Wilfred.

Gaspé nodded. "Come and look at him."

The two boys were soon watching earnestly through the grating, their faces almost touching. Gaspé's arm was over Wilfred's shoulder, as they drew closer and closer to each other.

Gaspé's grandfather took the slip of paper from his man, glanced at it, and crushed it in his hand. The chief was hastily heaping a mass of buffalo robes and skins and bags of pemmican upon one of the horses, a gift for the white man, horse and all. This was to show his big heart.

"Do you hear what he is saying?" whispered Gaspé, who understood the Indians much better than Wilfred did. "Listen!"

"Are there any Crees here? Crees have no manners. Crees are like dogs, always ready to bite if you turn your head away; but the Blackfeet have large hearts, and love hospitality."

"After all, those men in the reeds may only be on the watch for fear of a surprise from the Crees," continued Gaspé.

"Will there be a fight?" asked Wilfred breathlessly.

"No, I think not," answered Gaspé. "The Crees have lived amongst us whites so long they have given up the war-path. But," he added confidentially, "I have locked our old Indian in the kitchen, for if they

55

caught sight of him they might say we were friends of the Crees, and set on us."

One door in the white-painted house was standing open. It led into a large and almost empty room. Just inside it a number of articles were piled on the floor—a gun, blankets, scarlet cloth, and a brightly-painted canister of tea. Louison came back to fetch them, for a return present, with which the chief seemed highly delighted.

"We see but little of you white men," he said; "and our young men do not always know how to behave. But if you would come amongst us more, we chiefs would restrain them."

"He would have hard work," laughed Wilfred, little thinking how soon his words were to be verified. The Blackfeet standing round their chief, with their piles of skins, were so obviously getting excited, and impatient to begin the real trading, the chief must have felt even he could not hold them back much longer. But he was earnest in his exhortation to them not to give way to violence or rough behaviour.

Gaspé's grandfather was silently noting every face, without appearing to do so; and mindful of the warning he had received, he led the way to his gate, which he invited them to enter, observing, "My places are but small, friends. All shall come in by turns, but only a few at a time."

Gaspé drew back the bar and threw the gate wide. In walked the stately chief, with one or two of his followers who had taken part in the speech-making. The excited crowd at the back of them pushed their way in, as if they feared the gate might be shut in their faces.

Gaspé remonstrated, assuring them there was no hurry, all should have their turn.

The chief waved them back, and the last of the group contented themselves with standing in the gateway itself, to prevent it being shut against them.

Gaspé gave up the vain attempt to close it, and resumed his post.

"I am here on the watch," he whispered to Wilfred; "but you are cold and hungry. Go with grandfather into the shop."

"I would rather stay with you," answered Wilfred. "I am getting used to being hungry."

Gaspé answered this by pushing into his hand a big hunch of bread and

56

butter, which he had brought with him from his hurried breakfast.

Meanwhile Gaspé's grandfather had entered the house, taking with him the Blackfoot chief. He invited the others to enter and seat themselves on the floor of the empty room into which Wilfred had already had a peep. He unlocked an inner door, opening into a passage, which divided the great waiting-room from the small shop beyond. This had been carefully prepared for the reception of their wild customers. Only a few of his goods were left upon the shelves, which were arranged with much ingenuity, and seemed to display a great variety of wares, all of them attractive in Indian eyes. The bright-coloured cloths, cut in short lengths, were folded in fantastic heaps; the blankets were hung in graceful festoons. Beads scattered lightly on trays glittered behind the counter, on which the empty scales were lightly swaying up and down, like miniature swinging-boats.

A high lattice protected the front of the counter. Gaspé's grandfather established himself behind it. Louison took his place as door-keeper. The chief and two of his particular friends were the first to be admitted. Louison locked the door to keep out the others. It was the only way to preserve order. The wild, fierce strangers from the snow-covered plain and the darksome forest drew at once to the stove—a great iron box in the middle of the shop, with its huge black funnel rising through the ceiling. Warmth without smoke was a luxury unknown in the wigwam.

The Indians walked slowly round the shop, examining and considering the contents of the shelves, until their choice was made.

One of the three walked up to the counter and handed his pile of skins to the trader, Mr. De Brunier, through a little door in the lattice, pointing to some bright scarlet cloth and a couple of blankets. The chief was examining the guns. All three wanted shot, and the others inquired earnestly for the Indians' special delight, "tea and suga'." But when they saw the canister opened, and the tea poured into the scale, there was a grunt of dissatisfaction all round.

"What for?" demanded the chief. "Why put tea one side that swing and little bit of iron the other? Who wants little bit of iron? We don't know what that medicine is."

The Indians call everything medicine that seems to them learned and wise.

Mr. De Brunier tried to explain the use of his scales, and took up his steelyard to see if it would find more favour.

"Be fair," pursued the chief; "make one side as big as the other. Try bag of pemmican against your blankets and tea, then when the thing stops swinging you take pemmican, we blankets and tea—that fair!"

His companions echoed their chief's sentiments.

"As you like," smiled the trader. "We only want to make a fair exchange."

So the heavy bag of pemmican was put in the place of the weight, and a nice heap of tea was poured upon the blanket to make the balance true. The Indians were delighted.

"Now," continued Mr. De Brunier, "we must weigh the shot and the gun against your skins, according to your plan."

But when the red men saw their beautiful marten and otter and fisher skins piling higher and higher, and the heavy bag of shot still refusing to rise, a grave doubt as to the correctness of their own view of the matter arose in the Indians' minds. The first served took up his scarlet cloth and blanket and went out quickly, whilst the others deliberated.

The trader waited with good-humoured patience and a quiet gleam of amusement in the corner of his eye, when they told him at last to do it his own way, for the steel swing was a great medicine warriors could not understand. It was plain it could only be worked by some great medicine man like himself.

This decision had been reached so slowly, the impatience of the crowd in the waiting-room was at spirit-boil.

The brave who had come back satisfied was exhibiting his blankets and his scarlet cloth, which had to be felt and looked at by all in turn.

"Were there many more inside?" they asked eagerly.

He shook his head.

A belief that the good things would all be gone before the rest of the Indians could get their turn spread among the excited crowd like wild-fire.

Gaspé still held to his watch by the gate, with Wilfred beside him.

There was plenty of laughing and talking among the party of resolute men who kept it open; they seemed full of fun, and were joking each other in the highest spirits. Gaspé's eyes turned again and again to the frozen reeds, but all was quiet.

Wilfred was earnestly watching for a chance to ask the mirthful Blackfeet

58

if an old squaw, the Far-off-Dawn, had joined their camp. He could not make them understand him, but Gaspé repeated the question.

At that moment one of the fiercest-looking of the younger warriors rushed out of the waiting-room in a state of intense excitement. He beckoned to his companions at the gate, exclaiming, "If we don't help ourselves there will be nothing left for you and me."

"We know who will see fair play," retorted the young chief, who was answering Gaspé.

A whoop rang through the frosty air, and the still stiff reeds seemed suddenly alive with dusky faces. The crush round the inner door in the waiting-room became intense.

"Help me," whispered Gaspé, seizing Wilfred's arm and dragging him after him through the sheds to the back of the house. He took out a key and unlocked a side door. There was a second before him, with the keyhole at the reverse hand. It admitted them into a darkened room, for the windows were closely shuttered; but Gaspé knew his ground, and was not at a moment's loss.

The double doors were locked and bolted in double quick time behind them. Then Gaspé lifted up a heavy iron bar and banged it into its socket. Noise did not matter. The clamour in the waiting-room drowned every other sound.

"They will clear the shop," he said, "but we must stop them getting into the storeroom. Come along."

Wilfred was feeling the way. He stumbled over a chair; his hand felt a table. He guessed he was in the family sitting-room. Gaspé put his mouth to the keyhole of an inner door.

"Chirag!" he shouted to their Indian servant, "barricade."

The noises which succeeded showed that his command was being obeyed in that direction.

Gaspé was already in the storeroom, endeavouring to push a heavy box of nails before the other door leading into the shop. Wilfred was beside him in a moment. He had not much pushing power left in him after his night of wandering.

"Perhaps I can push a pound," he thought, laying his hands by Gaspé's.

"Now, steady! both together we shall do it," they said, and with one hard

59

strain the box was driven along the floor.

"That is something," cried Gaspé, heaving up a bag of ironmongery to put on the top of it. And he looked round for something else sufficiently ponderous to complete his barricade.

"What is this?" asked Wilfred, tugging at a chest of tools.

Meanwhile a dozen hatchets' heads were hammering at the door from the waiting-room where Louison was stationed. The crack of the wood giving way beneath their blows inspired Gaspé with redoubled energy. The chest was hoisted upon the box. He surveyed his barricade with satisfaction. But their work was not yet done. He dragged forward a set of steps, and running up to the top, threw open a trap-door in the ceiling. A ray of light streamed down into the room, showing Wilfred, very white and exhausted, leaning against the pile they had erected.

Gaspé sprang to the ground, rushed back into the sitting-room, and began to rummage in the cupboard.

"Here is grandfather's essence of peppermint and the sugar-basin and lots of biscuits!" he exclaimed. "You are faint, you have had no breakfast yet. I am forgetting. Here."

Wilfred's benumbed fingers felt in the sugar for a good-sized lump. Gaspé poured his peppermint drops upon it with a free hand. The warming, reviving dose brought back the colour to Wilfred's pale lips.

"Feel better?" asked his energetic companion, running up the steps with a roll of cloth on his shoulder, which he deposited safely in the loft above, inviting Wilfred to follow. The place was warm, for the iron chimneys ran through it, like so many black columns. Wilfred was ready to embrace the nearest.

Gaspé caught his arm. "You are too much of a human icicle for that," he cried. "I'll bring up the blankets next. Roll yourself up in them and get warm gradually, or you will be worse than ever. You must take care of yourself, for I dare not stop. It is always a bit dangerous when the Indians come up in such numbers to a little station like this. There is nobody but grandfather and me and our two men about the place, and what are four against a hundred? But all know what to do. Chirag watches inside the house, I outside, and Louison keeps the shop door. That is the most dangerous post, because of the crush to get in."

A crash and a thud in the room below verified his words.

"There! down it goes," he exclaimed, as a peal of laughter from many voices followed the rush of the crowd from one room to the other.

"They will be in here next," he added, springing down the steps for another load. Wilfred tried to shake off the strange sensations which oppressed him, and took it from him. Another and another followed quickly, until the boys had removed the greater part of the most valuable of the stores into the roof. The guns and the heavy bags of shot had all been carried up in the early morning, before the gate of the fort was opened.

And now the hammering began at the storeroom door, amid peals of uproarious laughter.

Gaspé tore up the steps with another heavy roll of bright blue cloth.

"We can do no more," he said, pausing for breath. "Now we will shut ourselves in here."

"We will have these up first," returned Wilfred, seizing hold of the top of the steps, and trying to drag them through the trap-door.

"Right!" ejaculated Gaspé. "If we had left them standing in the middle of the storeroom, it would have been inviting the Blackfeet to follow us."

They let down the trap-door as noiselessly as they could, and drew the heavy bolt at the very moment the door below was broken open and the triumphant crowd rushed wildly in, banging down their bags of pemmican on the floor, and seizing the first thing which came to hand in return.

Louison had been knocked down in the first rush from the waiting-room, and was leaning against the wall, having narrowly escaped being trampled to death. "All right!" he shouted to his master, who had jumped up on his counter to see if his agile servitor had regained his feet. It was wild work, but Mr. De Brunier took it all in good part, flinging his blankets right and left wherever he saw an eager hand outstretched to receive them. He knew that it was far better to give before they had time to take, and so keep up a semblance of trade. Many a beautiful skin and buffalo-robe was tossed across the counter in return. The heterogeneous pile was growing higher and higher beside him, and in the confusion it was hard to tell how much was intended for purchase, how much for pillage.

The chief, the Great Swan, as his people called him, still stood by the scales, determined to see if the great medicine worked fairly for all his people.

61

Mr. De Brunier called to him by his Indian name: "Oma-ka-pee-mulkee-yeu, do you not hear what I am saying? Your young men are too rough. Restrain them. You say you can. How am I to weigh and measure to each his right portion in such a rout?"

"Give them all something and they will be content," shouted the chief, trying his best to restore order.

Dozens of gaudy cotton handkerchiefs went flying over the black heads, scrambling with each other to get possession of them. Spoonfuls of beads were received with chuckles of delight by the nearest ranks; hut the Indians outside the crowd were growing hot and angry. Turns had been long since disregarded. It was catch as catch can. They broke down the lattice, and helped themselves from the shelves behind the counter. These were soon cleared. A party of strong young fellows, laughing as if it were the best fun in the world, leaped clear over the counter, and began to chop at the storeroom door with their hatchets. With a dexterous hand Mr. De Brunier flung his bright silks in their faces. The dancing skeins were quickly caught up. But the work of demolition went forward. The panels were reduced to matchwood. Three glittering hatchets swung high over the men's heads, came down upon the still resisting framework, and smashed it. The mirthful crowd dashed in.

The shop was already cleared. Mr. De Brunier would have gone into his storeroom with them if he could, but a dozen guns were pointed in his face. It was mere menace, no one attempted to fire. But the chief thought it was going too far. He backed to the waiting-room. Mr. De Brunier seized his empty tea-canister, and offered it to him as a parting gift, saying in most emphatic tones, "This is not our way of doing business. Some of these men have got too much, and some too little. It is not my fault. I must deal now with the tribe. Let them all lay down on the floor the rest of the skins and bags they have brought, and take away all I have to give in exchange, and you must divide when you get back to your camp, to every man his right share."

Oma-ka-pee-mulkee-yeu rushed off with his canister under his arm; not into the storeroom, where the dismayed trader hoped his presence might have proved a restraint, but straight through the waiting-room with a mad dash into the court, and through the gate, where he halted to give a thunderous shout of "Crees! Crees!" The magic words brought out his followers pell-mell. A second shout, a wilder alarm, made the tribe rally round their chief, in the full belief the Crees had surprised their camp in

62

their hateful dog-like fashion, taking their bite at the women and children when the warriors' heads were turned.

But the unmannerly foe was nowhere in sight.

"Over the hill!" shouted their Great Wild Swan, the man of twenty fights.

Meanwhile the gate of the little fort was securely barred against all intruders. The waiting squaws meekly turned their horses' heads, and followed their deluded lords, picking up the beads and nails which had been dropped in their headlong haste.

"Woe to Maxica," thought Wilfred, "if he should happen to be returning for his moose!"

The wild war-whoop died away in the distance, only the roar of the cataract broke the stillness of the snow-laden air.

De Brunier walked back into his house, to count up the gain and loss, and see how much reckless mischief that morning's work had brought him.

CHAPTER IX.

NEW FRIENDS.

"We shall always be friends," said Gaspé, looking into Wilfred's face, as they stood side by side against the chimney in the loft, emptying the biscuit-canister between them.

Wilfred answered with a sunny smile. The sounds below suddenly changed their character. The general stampede to the gate was beginning.

The boys flew to the window. It was a double one, very small and thickly frozen. They could not see the least thing through its glittering panes.

They could scarcely believe their ears, but the sudden silence which succeeded convinced Gaspé their rough visitors had beaten a hasty retreat.

"Anyhow we will wait a bit, and make sure before we go down," they decided.

But De Brunier's first care was for his grandson, and he was missing.

"Gaspard!" he shouted, and his call was echoed by Louison and Chirag.

"Here, grandfather; I am here, I am coming," answered the boy, gently raising the trap-door and peeping down at the dismantled storeroom. A great bag of goose-feathers, which had been hoarded by some thrifty squaw, had been torn open, and the down was flying in every direction.

63

There was a groan from Mr. De Brunier. All his most valuable stores had vanished.

"Not quite so bad as that, grandfather," cried Gaspé brightly.

The trader stepped up on to the remains of the barricade the boys had erected, and popped his head through the open trap-door.

"Well done, Gaspard!" he exclaimed.

"This other boy helped me," was the instantaneous reply.

The other boy came out from the midst of the blanket heap, feeling more dead than alive, and expecting every moment some one would say to him, "Now go," and he had nowhere to go.

Mr. De Brunier looked at him in amazement. A solitary boy in these lone wastes! Had he dropped from the skies?

"Come down, my little lad, and tell me who you are," he said kindly; but without waiting for a reply he walked on through the broken door to survey the devastation beyond.

"I have grown gray in the service of the Company, and never had a more provoking disaster," he lamented, as he began to count the tumbled heap of valuable furs blocking his pathway.

Louison, looking pale and feeling dizzy from his recent knock over, was collecting the bags of pemmican. Chirag, released from his imprisonment, was opening window shutters and replenishing the burnt-out fires. Gaspé dropped down from the roof, without waiting to replace the steps, and went to his grandfather's assistance, leaving Wilfred to have a good sleep in the blanket heap.

The poor boy was so worn out he slept heavily. When he roused himself at last, the October day was drawing to its close, and Gaspé was laughing beside him.

"Have not you had sleep enough?" he asked. "Would not dinner be an improvement?"

Wilfred wakened from his dreams of Acland's Hut. Aunt Miriam and Pena-Koam had got strangely jumbled together; but up he jumped to grasp his new friend's warm, young hand, and wondered what had happened. He felt as if he had been tossing like a ball from one strange scene to another. When he found himself sitting on a real chair, and not on the hard ground, the transition was so great it seemed like another dream.

64

The room was low, no carpet on the floor, only a few chairs ranged round the stove in the centre; but a real dinner, hot and smoking, was spread on the unpainted deal table.

Mr. De Brunier, with one arm thrown over the back of his chair, was smoking, to recall his lost serenity. An account-book lay beside his unfinished dinner. Sometimes his eye wandered over its long rows of figures, and then for a while he seemed absorbed in mental calculation.

He glanced at Wilfred's thin hands and pinched cheeks.

"Let the boy eat," he said to Gaspé.

As the roast goose vanished from Wilfred's plate the smile returned to his lips and the mirth to his heart. He outdid the hungry hunter of proverbial fame. The pause came at last; he could not quite keep on eating all night, Indian fashion. He really declined the sixth helping Gaspé was pressing upon him.

"No, thanks; I have had a Benjamin's portion—five times as much as you have had—and I am dreadfully obliged to you," said Wilfred, with a bow to Mr. De Brunier; "but there is Yula, that is my dog. May he have these bones?"

"He has had something more than bones already; Chirag fed him when he fed my puppies," put in Gaspé.

"Puppies," repeated Mr. De Brunier. "Dogs, I say."

"Not yet, grandfather," remonstrated the happy Gaspé. "You said they would not be really dogs, ready for work, until they were a year old, and it wants a full week."

"Please, sir," interrupted Wilfred abruptly, "can you tell me how I can get home?"

"Where is your home?" asked Mr. De Brunier.

"With my uncle, at Acland's Hut," answered Wilfred promptly.

"Acland's Hut," repeated Mr. De Brunier, looking across at Gaspé for elucidation. They did not know such a place existed.

"It is miles away from here," added Wilfred sorrowfully. "I went out hunting—"

"You—a small boy like you—to go hunting alone!" exclaimed Mr. De Brunier.

65

"Please, sir, I mean I rode on a pony by the cart which was to bring back the game," explained poor Wilfred, growing very rueful, as all hope of getting home again seemed to recede further and further from him. "The pony threw me," he added, "and when I came to myself the men were gone."

"Have you no father?" whispered Gaspé.

"My father died a year ago, and I was left at school at Garry," Wilfred went on.

"Fort Garry!" exclaimed Mr. De Brunier, brightening. "If this had happened a few weeks earlier, I could easily have sent you back to Garry in one of the Company's boats. They are always rowing up and down the river during the busy summer months, but they have just stopped for the winter With this Blackfoot camp so near us, I dare not unbar my gate again to-night, so make yourself contented. In the morning we will see what can be done."

"Nothing!" thought Wilfred, as he gathered the goose-bones together for Yula's benefit. "If you do not know where Acland's Hut is, and I cannot tell you, night or morning what difference can it make?"

He studied the table-cloth, thinking hard. "Bowkett and Diomé had talked of going to a hunters' camp. Where was that?"

"Ask Louison," said Mr. De Brunier, in reply to his inquiry.

Gaspé ran out to put the question.

Louison was a hunter's son. He had wintered in the camp himself when he was a boy. The hunters gathered there in November. Parties would soon be calling at the fort, to sell their skins by the way. Wilfred could go on with one of them, no doubt, and then Bowkett could take him home.

Wilfred's heart grew lighter. It was a roundabout-road, but he felt as if getting back to Bowkett was next to getting home.

"How glad your uncle will be to see you!" cried Gaspé radiantly, picturing the bright home-coming in the warmth of his own sympathy.

"Oh, don't!" said Wilfred; "please, don't. It won't be like that; not a bit. Nobody wants me. Aunt wanted my little sister, not me. You don't understand; I am such a bother to her."

Gaspé was silenced, but his hand clasped Wilfred's a little closer. All the chivalrous feelings of the knightly De Bruniers were rousing in his breast for the strange boy who had brought them the timely warning. For some of the best and noblest blood of old France was flowing in his veins. A De Brunier had come out with the early French settlers, the first explorers, the first voyageurs along the mighty Canadian rivers. A De Brunier had fought against Wolfe on the Heights of Abraham, in the front ranks of that gallant band who faithfully upheld their nation's honour, loyal to the last to the shameless France, which despised, neglected, and abandoned them—men whose high sense of duty never swerved in the hour of trial, when they were given over into the hands of their enemy. Who cared what happened in that far-off corner of the world? It was not worth troubling about. So the France of that day reasoned when she flung them from her.

It was of those dark hours Gaspé loved to make his grandfather talk, and he was thinking that nothing would divert Wilfred from his troubled thoughts like one of grandfather's stories. The night drew on. The snow was falling thicker and denser than before. Mr. De Brunier turned his chair to the stove, afraid to go to bed with the Blackfoot camp within half-a-mile of his wooden walls.

"They might," he said, "have a fancy to give us a midnight scare, to see what more they could get."

The boys begged hard to remain. The fire, shut in its iron box, was burning at its best, emitting a dull red glow, even through its prison walls. Gaspé refilled his grandfather's pipe.

"Wilfred," he remarked gently, "has a home that is no home, and he thinks we cannot understand the ups and downs of life, or what it is to be pushed to the wall."

Gaspé had touched the right spring. The veteran trader smiled. "Not know, my lad, what it is to be pushed to the wall, when I have been a servant for fifty years in the very house where my grandfather was master, before the golden lilies on our snow-white banner were torn down to make room for your Union Jack! Why am I telling you this to-night? Just to show you, when all seems lost in the present, there is the future beyond, and no one can tell what that may hold. The pearl lies hidden under the stormiest waters. Do you know old Cumberland House? A De Brunier built it, the first trading-fort in the Saskatchewan. It was lost to us when the cold-hearted Bourbon flung us like a bone to the English mastiff. Our homes were ours no longer. Our lives were in our hands, but our honour no one but ourselves could throw away. What did we do? What could we do? What all can do—our duty to the last. We braved our trouble; and

67

when all seemed lost, help came. Who was it felt for us? The men who had torn from us our colours and entered our gates by force. Under the British flag our homes were given back, our rights assured. Our Canadian Quebec remains unaltered, a transplant from the old France of the Bourbons. In the long years that have followed the harvest has been reaped on both sides. Now, my boy, don't break your heart with thinking, If there had been anybody to care for me, I should not have been left senseless in a snow-covered wilderness; but rouse your manhood and face your trouble, for in God's providence it may be more than made up to you. Here you can stay until some opportunity occurs to send you to this hunters' camp. You are sure it will be your best way to get home again?"

"Yes," answered Wilfred decidedly. "I shall find Bowkett there, and I am sure he will take me back to Acland's Hut. But please, sir, I did not mean aunt and uncle were unkind; but I had been there such a little while, and somehow I was always wrong; and then I know I teased."

The cloud was gathering over him again.

"If—" he sighed.

"Don't dwell on the *ifs*, my boy; talk of what has been. That will teach you best what may be," inter posed Mr. De Brunier.

Gaspé saw the look of pain in Wilfred's eyes, although he did not say again, "Please don't talk about it," for he was afraid Mr. De Brunier would not call that facing his trouble.

Gaspé came to the rescue. "But, grandfather, you have not told us what the harvest was that Canada reaped," he put in.

"Cannot you see it for yourself, Gaspard?" said Mr. De Brunier. "When French and English, conquered and conqueror, settled down side by side, it was their respect for each other, their careful consideration for each other's rights and wrongs, that taught their children and their children's children the great lesson how to live and let live. No other nation in the world has learned as we have done. It is this that makes our Canada a land of refuge for the down-trodden slave. And we, the French in Canada, what have we reaped?" he went on, shaking the ashes from his pipe, and looking at the two boys before him, French and English; but the old lines were fading, and uniting in the broader name of Canadian. "Yes," he repeated, "what did we find at the bottom of our bitter cup? Peace, security, and freedom, whilst the streets of Paris ran red with Frenchmen's blood. The last De Brunier in France was dragged from his ancestral home to the steps of the guillotine by Frenchmen's hands, and the old chateau in Brittany is left a moss-grown ruin. When my father saw the hereditary foe of his country walk into Cumberland House to turn him out, they met with a bonjour [good day]; and when they parted this was the final word: 'You are a young man, Monsieur De Brunier, but your knowledge of the country and your influence with the Indians can render us valuable assistance. If at any time you choose to take office in your old locale, you will find that faithful service will be handsomely requited.' We kept our honour and laid down our pride. Content. Your British Queen has no more loyal subjects in all her vast dominions than her old French Canadians."

There was a mist before Wilfred's eyes, and his voice was low and husky. He only whispered, "I shall not forget, I never can forget to-night."

The small hours of the morning were numbered before Gaspé opened the door of his little sleeping room, which Wilfred was to share. It was not much bigger than a closet. The bed seemed to fill it.

There was just room for Gaspé's chest of clothes and an array of pegs. But to Wilfred it seemed a palace, in its cozy warmth. It made him think of Pe-na-Koam. He hoped she was as comfortable in the Blackfoot camp.

Gaspé was growing sleepy. One arm was round Wilfred's neck; he roused himself to answer, "Did not you hear what the warrior with the scalps at his belt told me? She came into their camp, and they gave her food as long as she could eat it. She was too old to travel, and they left her asleep by their camp-fires."

Up sprang Wilfred. "Whatever shall I do? I have brought away her kettle; I thought she had gone to her own people, and left it behind her for me."

"Do!" repeated Gaspé, laughing. "Why, go to sleep old fellow; what else can we do at four o'clock in the morning? If we don't make haste about it, we shall have no night at all."

Gaspé was quick to follow his own advice. But the "no night" was Wilfred's portion. There was no rest for him for thinking of Pe-na-Koam. How was she to get her breakfast? The Blackfeet might have given her food, but how could she boil a drop of water without her kettle?

At the first movement in the house he slipped out of bed and dressed himself. The fire had burned low in the great stove in the sitting-room, but when he softly opened the door of their closet it struck fairly warm. The

69

noise he had heard was Louison coming in with a great basket of wood to build it up.

"A fire in prison is a dull affair by daylight," remarked Wilfred. "I think I shall go for a walk—a long walk."

"Mr. De Brunier will have something to say about that after last night's blizzard," returned Louison.

"Then please tell him it is my duty to go, for I am afraid an old Indian woman, who was very kind to me, was out in last night's snow, and I must go and look for her. Will you just undo that door and let me out?"

"Not quite so fast; I have two minds about that," answered Louison. "Better wait for Mr. De Brunier. I know I shall be wrong if I let you go off like this."

"How can you be wrong?" retorted Wilfred. "I came to this place to warn you all there was a party of Blackfeet hidden in the reeds. Well, if I had waited, what good would it have been to you? Now I find the old squaw who made me these gloves was out in last night's snow, and I must go and look for her, and go directly."

"But a boy like you will never find her," laughed Louison.

"I'll try it," said Wilfred doggedly.

"Was she a Blackfoot?"

"Yes."

"Then she is safe enough in camp, depend upon it," returned Louison.

"No, she was left behind," persisted Wilfred.

"Then come with me," said Louison, by no means sorry to have found a friendly reason for approaching the Blackfeet camp. "I have a little bit of scout business in hand, just to find out whether these wild fellows are moving on, or whether they mean waiting about to pay us another visit."

Chirag was clearing away the snow in the enclosure outside. Wilfred found the kettle and the skin just where he had laid them down, inside the first shed. He called up Yula, and started by Louison's side. Chirag was waiting to bar the gate behind them.

"Beautiful morning," said the Canadians, vigorously rubbing their noses to keep them from freezing, and violently clapping their mittened hands together. The snow lay white and level, over hill and marsh, one sparkling

70

sheet of silvery sheen. The edging of ice was broadening along the river, and the roar of the falls came with a thunderous boom through the all-pervading stillness around them.

The snow was already hard, as the two ran briskly forward, with Yula careering and bounding in extravagant delight.

Wilfred looked back to the little fort, with its stout wooden walls, twice the height of a man, hiding the low white house with its roof of bark, hiding everything within but the rough lookout and the tall flag-staff, for

"Ever above the topmost roof the banner of England blew."

Wilfred was picturing the feelings with which the De Bruniers had worked on beneath it, giving the same faithful service to their foreign masters that they had to the country which had cast them off.

"It is a dirty old rag," said Louison; "gone all to ribbons in last night's gale. But it is good enough for a little place like this—we call it Hungry Hall. We don't keep it open all the year round. Just now, in October, the Indians and the hunters are bringing in the produce of their summer's hunting. We shall shut up soon, and open later again for the winter trade."

"A dirty old rag!" repeated Wilfred. "Yes, but I am prouder of it than ever, for it means protection and safety wherever it floats. Boy as I am, I can see that."

"Can you see something else," asked Louison—"the crossing poles of the first wigwam? We are at the camp."

CHAPTER X.

THE DOG-SLED.

A cloud of smoke from its many wigwam fires overhung the Indian camp as Louison and Wilfred drew near. The hunter's son, with his quick ear, stole cautiously through the belt of pine trees which sheltered it from the north wind, listening for any sounds of awakening life. Yesterday's adventure had no doubt been followed by a prolonged feast, and men and dogs were still sleeping. A few squaws, upon whom the hard work of the Indian world all devolves, were already astir. Louison thought they were gathering firewood outside the camp. This was well. Louison hung round about the outskirts, watching their proceedings, until he saw one woman behind a wigwam gathering snow to fill her kettle. Her pappoose in its wooden cradle was strapped to her back; but she had seen or heard them,

71

for she paused in her occupation and looked up wondering.

Louison stepped forward.

"Now for your questions, my boy," he said to Wilfred, "and I will play interpreter."

"Is there an old squaw in your camp named the Far-off-Dawn?"

Wilfred needed no interpreter to explain the "caween" given in reply.

"Tell her, Louison," he hurried on, "she was with me the night before last. I thought she left me to follow this trail. If she has not reached this camp, she must be lost in the snow."

"Will not some of your people go and look for her," added Louison, on his own account, "before you move on?"

"What is the use?" she asked. "Death will have got her by this time. She came to the camp; she was too old to travel. If she is alive, she may overtake us again. We shall not move on until another sunrising, to rest the horses."

"Then I shall go and look for her," said Wilfred resolutely.

"Not you," retorted Louison; "wait a bit." He put his hand in his pockets. They had been well filled with tea and tobacco, in readiness for any emergency. "Is not there anybody in the camp who will go and look for her?"

Louison was asking his questions for the sake of the information he elicited, but Wilfred caught at the idea in earnest. "Go and see," urged Louison, offering her a handful of his tea.

"Thé!" she repeated. The magic word did wonders. Louison knew if one of the men were willing to leave the camp to look for Pe-na-Koam, no further mischief was intended. But if they were anticipating a repetition of "the high old time" they had enjoyed yesterday, not one of them could be induced to forego their portion in so congenial a lark, for in their eyes it was nothing more.

The squaw took the tea in both her hands, gladly leaving her kettle in the snow, as she led the way into the camp.

Wilfred, who had only seen the poor little canvas tents of the Crees, looked round him in astonishment. In the centre stood the lodge or moya of the chief—a wigwam built in true old Indian style, fourteen feet high at the least. Twelve strong poles were stuck in the ground, round a circle fifteen feet across. They were tied together at the top, and the outside was covered with buffalo-skins, painted black and red in all sorts of figures. Eagles seemed perching on the heads of deers, and serpents twisted and coiled beneath the feet of buffaloes. The other wigwams built around it were in the same style, on a smaller scale, all brown with smoke.

A goodly array of spears, bows, and shields adorned the outside of the moya; above them the much-coveted rifles were ranged with exceeding pride. The ground between the moya and the tents was littered with chips and bones, among which the dogs were busy. A few children were pelting each other with the snow, or trying to shoot at the busy jays with a baby of a bow and arrows to match.

Louison pushed aside the fur which hung over the entrance to the moya— the man-hole—and stepped inside. A beautiful fire was burning in the middle of the tent. The floor was strewed with pine brush, and skins were hung round the inside wall, like a dado. They fitted very closely to the ground, so as to keep out all draught. The rabbits and swans, the buzzards and squirrels painted on this dado were so lifelike, Wilfred thought it must be as good as a picture-book to the dear little pappoose, strapped to its flat board cradle, and set upright against the wall whilst mother was busy. The sleeping-places were divided by wicker-screens, and seemed furnished with plenty of blankets and skins. One or two of them were still occupied; but Oma-ka-pee-mulkee-yeu lay on a bear-skin by the fire, with his numerous pipes arranged beside him. The squaw explained the errand of their early visitors: a woman was lost in the snow, would the chief send one of his people to find her?

The Great Swan looked over his shoulder and said something. A young man rose up from one of the sleeping-places.

Both were asking, "What was the good?"

"She is one of your own people," urged Louison. "We came to tell you."

This was not what Wilfred had said, and it was not all he wanted, but he was forced to trust it to Louison, although he was uneasy.

He could see plainly enough an Indian would be far more likely to find her than himself, but would they? Would any of them go?

Louison offered a taste of his tobacco to the old chief and the young, by way of good-fellowship.

73

"They will never do it for that," thought Wilfred growing desperate again. He had but one thing about him he could offer as an inducement, and that was his knife. He hesitated a moment. He thought of Pe-na-Koam dying in the snow, and held it out to the young chieftain.

The dusky fingers gripped the handle.

"Will you take care of her and bring her here, or give her food and build up her hut?" asked Wilfred, making his meaning as plain as he could, by the help of nods and looks and signs.

The young chief was outside the man-hole in another moment. He slung his quiver to his belt and took down his bow, flung a stout blanket over his shoulder, and shouted to his squaw to catch a bronco, the usual name for the Canadian horse. The kettle was in his hand.

"Can we trust him?" asked Wilfred, as he left the camp by Louison's side.

"Trust him! yes," answered his companion. "Young Sapoo is one of those Indians who never break faith. His word once given, he will keep it to the death."

"Then I have only to pray that he may be in time," said Wilfred gravely, as he stood still to watch the wild red man galloping back to the beavers' lakelet.

"Oh, he will be in time," returned Louison cheerily. "All their wigwam poles would be left standing, and plenty of pine brush and firewood strewing about. She is sure to have found some shelter before the heaviest fall of snow; that did not come until it was nearly morning."

Gaspé had climbed the lookout to watch for their return.

"Wilfred, *mon cher*," he exclaimed, "you must have a perfect penchant for running away. How could you give us the slip in such a shabby fashion? I could not believe Chirag. If the bears were not all dropping off into their winter sleep, I should have thought some hungry bruin had breakfasted upon you."

Gaspé's grandfather had turned carpenter, and was already at work mending his broken doors. Not being a very experienced workman, his planking and his panelling did not square. Wood was plentiful, and more than one piece was thrown aside as a misfit. Both the boys were eager to assist in the work of restoration. A broken shelf was mended between them—in first-rate workmanly style, as Wilfred really thought. "We have done that well," they agreed; and when Mr. De Brunier—who was still

74

chipping at his refractory panel—added a note of commendation to their labours, Gaspé's spirits ran up to the very top of the mental thermometer.

To recover his balance—for Wilfred unceremoniously declared he was off his head—Gaspé fell into a musing fit. He wakened up, exclaiming,—

"I'm flying high!"

"Then mind you don't fall," retorted Mr. De Brunier, who himself was cogitating somewhat darkly over Louison's intelligence. "There will be no peace for me," he said, "no security, whilst these Blackfeet are in the neighbourhood. 'Wait for another sun-rising'—that means another forty-eight hours of incessant vigilance for me. It was want of confidence did it all. I should teach them to trust me in time, but it cannot be done in a day."

As he moved on, lamenting over the scene of destruction, Gaspé laid a hand on Wilfred's arm. "How are you going to keep pace with the hunters with that lame foot?" he demanded.

"As the tortoise did with the hare," laughed Wilfred. "Get myself left behind often enough, I don't doubt that."

"But I doubt if you will ever get to your home *à la tortoise*," rejoined Gaspé. "No, walking will never do for you. I am thinking of making you a sled."

"A sledge!" repeated Wilfred in surprise.

"Oh, we drop the 'ge' you add to it in your English dictionaries," retorted Gaspé. "We only say sled out here. There will be plenty of board when grandfather has done his mending. We may have what we want, I'm sure. Your dog is a trained hauler, and why shouldn't we teach my biggest pup to draw with him? They would drag you after the hunters in fine style. We can do it all, even to their jingling bells."

Wilfred, who had been accustomed to the light and graceful carioles and sledges used in the Canadian towns, thought it was flying a bit too high. But Gaspé, up in all the rough-and-ready contrivances of the backwoods, knew what he was about. Louison and Chirag had to be consulted.

When all the defences were put in order—bolts, bars, and padlocks doubled and trebled, and a rough but very ponderous double door added to the storeroom—Mr. De Brunier began to speak of rest.

"The night cometh in which no man can work," he quoted, as if in

75

justification of the necessary stoppage.

The hammer was laid down, and he sank back in his hard chair, as if he were almost ashamed to indulge in his one solace, the well-filled pipe Gaspé was placing so coaxingly in his fingers. A few sedative whiffs were enjoyed in silence; but before the boys were sent off to bed, Gaspé had secured the reversion of all the wooden remains of the carpentering bout, and as many nails as might be reasonably required.

"Now," said Gaspé, as he tucked himself up by Wilfred's side, and pulled the coverings well over head and ears, "I'll show you what I can do."

Three days passed quickly by. On the morning of the fourth Louison walked in with a long face. The new horse, the gift of the Blackfoot chief, had vanished in the night. The camp had moved on, nothing but the long poles of the wigwams were left standing.

The loss of a horse is such an everyday occurrence in Canada, where horses are so often left to take care of themselves, it was by no means clear that Oma-ka-pee-mulkee-yeu had resumed his gift, but it was highly probable.

Notwithstanding, the Company had not been losers by the riotous marketing, for the furs the Blackfeet had brought in were splendid.

"Yes, we were all on our guard—thanks to you, my little man—or it might have ended in the demolition of the fort," remarked Mr. De Brunier. "Now, if there is anything you want for your journey, tell me, and you shall have it."

"Yes, grandfather," interposed Gaspé. "He must have a blanket to sleep in, and there is the harness for the dogs, and a lot of things."

Wilfred grew hot. "Please, sir, thanks; but I don't think I want much. Most of all, perhaps, something to eat."

Mr. De Brunier recommended a good hunch of pemmican, to cut and come again. The hunters would let him mess with them if he brought his own pemmican and a handful of tea to throw into their boiling kettle. The hunters' camp was about sixty miles from Hungry Hall. They would be two or three days on the road.

More than one party of hunters had called at the fort already, wanting powder and ball, matches, and a knife; and when the lynx and marten and wolf skins which they brought were told up, and the few necessaries they required were provided, the gay, careless, improvident fellows would invest in a tasselled cap bright with glittering beads.

The longer Wilfred stayed at the fort, the more Mr. De Brunier hesitated about letting the boy start for so long a journey with no better protection. Gaspard never failed to paint the danger and magnify the difficulties of the undertaking, wishing to keep his new friend a little longer. But Wilfred was steady to his purpose. He saw no other chance of getting back to his home. He did not say much when Mr. De Brunier and Gaspé were weighing chances and probabilities, hoping some travelling party from the north might stop by the way at Hungry Hall and take him on with them. Such things did happen occasionally.

But Wilfred had a vivid recollection of his cross-country journey with Forgill. He could not see that he should be sure of getting home if he accepted Mr. De Brunier's offer and stayed until the river was frozen and then went down with him to their mid-winter station, trusting to a seat in some of the Company's carts or the Company's sledges to their next destination.

Then there would be waiting and trusting again to be sent on another stage, and another, and another, until he would at last find himself at Fort Garry. "Then," he asked, "what was he to do? If his uncle and aunt knew that he was there, they might send Forgill again to fetch him. But if letters reached Acland's Hut so uncertainly, how was he to let them know?"

As Wilfred worked the matter out thus in his own mind, he received every proposition of Mr. De Brunier's with, "Please, sir, I'd rather go to Bowkett. He lost me. He will be sure to take me straight home."

"The boy knew his own mind so thoroughly," Mr. De Brunier told Gaspard at last, "they must let him have his own way."

The sled was finished. It was a simple affair—two thin boards about four feet long nailed together edgeways, with a tri-cornered piece of wood fitted in at the end. Two old skates were screwed on the bottom, and the thing was done. The boys worked together at the harness as they sat round the stove in the evening. The snow was thicker, the frost was harder every night. Ice had settled on the quiet pools, and was spreading over the quick-running streams, but the dash of the falls still resisted its ever-encroaching influence. By-and-by they too must yield, and the whole face of nature would be locked in its iron clasp. November was wearing away. A sunny morning came now and then to cheer the little party so soon to separate.

Gaspé proposed a run with the dogs, just to try how they would go in their new harness, and if, after all, the sled would run as a sled should.

Other things were set aside, and boys and men gathered in the court. Even Mr. De Brunier stepped out to give his opinion about the puppies. Gaspé had named them from the many tongues of his native Canada.

In his heart Wilfred entertained a secret belief that not one of them would ever be equal to his Yula. They were Athabascans. They would never be as big for one thing, and no dog ever could be half as intelligent; that was not possible. But he did not give utterance to these sentiments. It would have looked so ungrateful, when Gaspé was designing the best and biggest for his parting gift. And they were beauties, all four of them.

There was Le Chevalier, so named because he never appeared, as Gaspé declared, without his white shirtfront and white gloves. Then there was his bluff old English Boxer, the sturdiest of the four. He looked like a hauler. Kusky-tay-ka-atim-moos, or "the little black dog," according to the Cree dialect, had struck up a friendship with Yula, only a little less warm than that which existed between their respective masters. Then the little schemer with the party-coloured face was Yankee-doodle.

"Try them all in harness, and see which runs the best," suggested grandfather, quite glad that his Gaspard should have one bright holiday to checker the leaden dulness of the everyday life at Hungry Hall.

Louison was harnessing the team. He nailed two long strips of leather to the lowest end of the sled for traces. The dogs' collars were made of soft leather, and slipped over the head. Each one was ornamented with a little tinkling bell under the chin and a tuft of bright ribbon at the back of the ear, and a buckle on either side through which the traces were passed. A band of leather round the dogs completed the harness, and to this the traces were also securely buckled. The dogs stood one before the other, about a foot apart.

Yula was an experienced hand, and took the collar as a matter of course. Yankee was the first of the puppies to stand in the traces, and his severe doggie tastes were completely outraged by the amount of finery Gaspé and Louison seemed to think necessary for their proper appearance.

Wilfred was seated on a folded blanket, with a buffalo-robe tucked over his feet. Louison flourished a whip in the air to make the dogs start. Away went Yula with something of the velocity of an arrow from a bow, knocking down Gaspé, who thought of holding the back of the sled to guide it.

He scrambled to his feet and ran after it. Yula was careering over the snow at racehorse speed, ten miles an hour, and poor little Yankee, almost frightened out of his senses, was bent upon making a dash at the ribbon waving so enticingly before his eyes. He darted forward. He hung back. He lurched from side to side. He twisted, he turned. He upset the equilibrium of the sledge. It banged against a tree on one side, and all but tilted over on the other. One end went down into a badger hole, leaving Wilfred and his blanket in a heap on the snow, when Yankee, lightened of half his load, fairly leaped upon Yula's back and hopelessly entangled the traces. The boys concealed an uneasy sense of ignominious failure under an assertion calculated to put as good a face as they could on the matter: "We have not got it quite right yet, but we shall."

CHAPTER XI.

THE HUNTERS' CAMP.

A burst of merry laughter made the two boys look round, half afraid that it might be at their own expense.

Wilfred felt a bit annoyed when he perceived a little party of horsemen spurring towards the fort. But Gaspé ran after them, waving his arms with a bonjour as he recognized his own Louison's cousin, Batiste, among the foremost.

Dog training and dog driving are the never-failing topics of interest among the hunters and trappers. Batiste had reined in his horse to watch the ineffectual efforts of the boys to disentangle the two dogs, who were fighting and snarling with each other over the upturned sled.

Batiste and his comrades soon advanced from watching to helping. The sled was lifted up, the traces disentangled, and Wilfred and Gaspé were told and made to feel that they knew nothing at all about dog driving, and might find themselves in a heap all pell-mell at the bottom of the river bank some day if they set about it in such a reckless fashion. They were letting the dogs run just where they liked. Dogs wanted something to follow. Batiste jumped from his horse at last, quite unable to resist the pleasure of breaking in a young dog.

"It takes two to manage a dog team," he asserted. "It wants a man in snow-shoes to walk on in front and mark a track, and another behind to keep them steady to their work."

Dogs, horses, men, and boys all turned back together to discuss Yankee's

79

undeveloped powers. But no, Batiste himself could do nothing with him. Yankee refused to haul.

"I'll make him," said Batiste.

But Gaspé preferred to take his dog out of the traces rather than surrender him to the tender mercies of a hunter. "I know they are very cruel," he whispered to Wilfred. So Yula was left to draw the empty sled back to the fort, and he did it in first-rate style.

"He is just cut out for hauling, as the hound is for hunting," explained Batiste. "It is not any dog can do it."

They entered the gate of the fort. The men stood patting and praising Yula, while Batiste exchanged greetings with his cousin.

Before he unlocked the door of his shop, Mr. De Brunier called Wilfred to him.

"Now is your chance, my boy," he said kindly. "Batiste tells me he passed this Bowkett on his way to the camp, so you are sure to find him there. Shall I arrange with Batiste to take you with him?"

The opportunity had come so suddenly at last. If Wilfred had any misgiving, he did not show it.

"What do you think I had better do, sir?" he asked.

"There is so much good common sense in your own plan," answered his friend, "I think you had better follow it. When we shut up, you cannot remain here; and unless we take you with us, this is the best thing to do."

Wilfred put both his hands in Mr. De Brunier's.

"I can't thank you," he said; "I can't thank you half enough."

"Never mind the thanks, my boy. Now I want you to promise me, when you get back to your home, you will make yourself missed, then you will soon find yourself wanted." Mr. De Brunier turned the key in the lock as he spoke, and went in.

Wilfred crossed the court to Gaspé. He looked up brightly, exclaiming, "Kusky is the boy for you; they all say Kusky will draw."

"I am going," whispered Wilfred.

"Going! how and why?" echoed Gaspé in consternation.

"With these men," answered Wilfred.

80

"Then I shall hate Batiste if he takes you from me!" exclaimed Gaspé impetuously.

They stepped back into the shed the puppies had occupied, behind some packing-cases, where nobody could see them, for the parting words.

"We shall never forget each other, never. Shall we ever meet again?" asked Wilfred despairingly. "We may when we are men."

"We may before," whispered Gaspé, trying to comfort him. "Grandfather's time is up this Christmas. Then he will take his pension and retire. He talks of buying a farm. Why shouldn't it be near your uncle's?"

"Come, Gaspard, what are you about?" shouted Mr. De Brunier from the shop door. "Take Wilfred in, and see that he has a good dinner."

Words failed over the knife and fork. Yula and Kusky had to be fed.

"Will the sled be of any use?" asked Gaspé.

Even Wilfred did not feel sure. They had fallen very low—had no heart for anything.

Louison was packing the sled—pemmican and tea for three days.

"Put plenty," said Gaspé, as he ran out to see all was right.

Louison and Batiste were talking.

"We'll teach that young dog to haul," Batiste was saying; "and if the boy gets tired of them, we'll take them off his hands altogether."

"With pleasure," added Louison, and they both laughed.

The last moment had come.

"Good-bye, good-bye!" said Wilfred, determined not to break down before the men, who were already mounting their horses.

"God bless you!" murmured Gaspé.

Batiste put Wilfred on his horse, and undertook the management of the sled. The unexpected pleasure of a ride helped to soften the pain of parting.

"I ought to be thankful," thought Wilfred—"I ought to rejoice that the chance I have longed for has come. I ought to be grateful that I have a home, and such a good home." But it was all too new. No one had learned to love him there. Whose hand would clasp his when he reached Acland's

Hut as Gaspé had done?

On, on, over the wide, wild waste of sparkling snow, with his jovial companions laughing and talking around him. It was so similar to his ride with Bowkett and Diomé, save for the increase in the cold. He did not mind that.

But there was one thing Wilfred did mind, and that was the hard blows Batiste was raining down on Kusky and Yula. He sprang down to remonstrate. He wanted to drive them himself. He was laughed at for a self-conceited jackass, and pushed aside.

Dog driving was the hunter's hobby. The whole party were engrossed in watching Yula's progress, and quiet, affectionate little Kusky's infantine endeavours to keep up with him.

Batiste regarded himself as a crack trainer, and when poor Kusky brought the whole cavalcade to a standstill by sitting down in the midst of his traces, he announced his intention of curing him of such a trick with his first taste.

"Send him to Rome," shouted one of the foremost of the hunters. "He'll not forget that in a hurry."

"He is worth training well," observed another. "See what a chest he has. He will make as good a hauler as the old one by-and-by. Pay him well first start."

What "sending to Rome" might mean Wilfred did not stay to see. Enough to know it was the uttermost depth of dog disgrace. He saw Batiste double up his fist and raise his arm. The sprain in his ankle was forgotten. He flew to the ground, and dashed between Batiste and his dogs, exclaiming, "They are mine, my own, and they shan't be hurt by anybody!"

He caught the first blow, that was all. He staggered backwards on the slippery ground.

Another of the hunters had alighted. He caught Wilfred by the arm, and pulled him up, observing dryly, "Well done, young 'un. Got a settler unawares. That just comes of interfering.—Here, Mathurin, take him up behind ye."

The hunter appealed to wheeled round with a good-natured laugh.

But Wilfred could not stand; the horses, dogs, and snow seemed dancing round him.

"Yula! Kusky!" he called, like one speaking in a dream.

But Yula, dragging the sled behind him, and rolling Kusky over and over in the tangling harness, had sprung at Batiste's arm; but he was too hampered to seize him. Wilfred was only aware of a confused *mêlée* as he was hoisted into Mathurin's strong arms and trotted away from the scene of action.

"Come, you are the sauciest young dog of the three," said Mathurin rather admiringly. "There, lay your head on me. You'll have to sleep this off a bit," he continued, gently walking his horse, and gradually dropping behind the rest of the party.

Poor Wilfred roused up every now and then with a rather wild and incoherent inquiry for his dogs, to which Mathurin replied with a drawling, sleepy-sounding "All right."

Wilfred's eyes were so swollen over that he hardly knew it was starshine when Mathurin laid him down by a new-lit camping-fire.

"There," said the hunter, in the self-congratulatory tone of a man who knows he has got over an awkward piece of business; "let him have his dogs, and give him a cup of tea, and he'll be himself again by the morning."

"Ready for the same game?" asked Batiste, who was presiding over the tea-kettle.

The cup which Mathurin recommended was poured out; the sugar was not spared. Wilfred drank it gladly without speaking. When words were useless silence seemed golden. Yula was on guard beside him, and poor little Kusky, cowed and cringing, was shivering at his feet. They covered him up, and all he had seen and heard seemed as unreal as his dreams.

The now familiar cry of "*Lève! lève!*" made Yula sit upright. The hunters were astir before the dawn, but Wilfred was left undisturbed for another hour at least, until the rubeiboo was ready—that is, pemmican boiled in water until it makes a sort of soup. Pemmican, as Mr. De Brunier had said, was the hunters' favourite food.

"Now for the best of the breakfast for the lame and tame," laughed Batiste, pulling up Wilfred, and looking at his disfiguring bruises with a whistle.

Wilfred shrank from the prospect before him. Another day of bitter biting cold, and merciless cruelty to his poor dogs. "Oh, if Gaspé knew!—if

83

Kusky could but have run back home!"

Wilfred could not eat much. He gave his breakfast to his dogs, and fondled them in silence. It was enough to make a fellow's blood boil to be called Mathurin's babby, *l'enfant endormi* (sleepy child), and Pierre the pretty face.

"Can we be such stoics, Yula," he whispered, "as to stand all this another twenty-four hours, and see our poor little Kusky beaten right and left? Can we bear it till to-morrow morning?"

Yula washed the nervous fingers stroking his hair out of his eyes, and looked the picture of patient endurance. There was no escape, but it could not last long. Wilfred set his teeth, and asserted no one but himself should put the harness on his dogs.

"Gently, my little turkey-cock," put in Mathurin. "The puppy may be your own, but the stray belongs to a friend of mine, who will be glad enough to see him back again."

Wilfred was fairly frightened now. "Oh, if he had to give his Yula chummie back to some horrid stranger!" He thought it would be the last straw which brings the breakdown to boy as well as camel. But he consoled himself at their journey's end. Bowkett would interfere on his behalf. Mathurin's assertion was not true, by the twinkle in his eye and the laugh to his companions. Louison must have told his cousin that Yula was a stray, or they would never have guessed it. True or false, the danger of losing his dog was a real one. They meant to take it from him. One thing Wilfred had the sense to see, getting in a passion was of no good anyway. "Frederick the Great lost his battle when he lost his temper," he thought. "Keep mine for Yula's sake I will."

But the work was harder than he expected, although the time was shorter. The hardy broncos of the hunters were as untiring as their masters. Ten, twenty, thirty miles were got over without a sign of weariness from any one but Wilfred and Kusky. If they were dead beat, what did it matter? The dog was lashed along, and Wilfred was teased, to keep him from falling asleep.

"One more push," said the hunters, "and instead of sleeping with our feet to a camp-fire, and our beards freezing to the blankets, we shall be footing it to Bowkett's fiddle."

The moon had risen clear and bright above the sleeping clouds still darkening the horizon. A silent planet burned lamp-like in the western sky. Forest and prairie, ridges and lowland, were sparkling in the sheen of the moonlight and the snow.

Wilfred roused himself. The tinkle of the dog-bells was growing fainter and fainter, as Mathurin galloped into the midst of a score or so of huts promiscuously crowded together, while many a high-piled meat-stage gave promise of a winter's plenty. Huge bones and horns, the remnants of yesterday's feast, were everywhere strewing the ground, and changing its snowy carpet to a dingy drab. There were wolf-skins spread over framework. There were buffalo-skins to be smoked, and buffalo-robes—as they are called when the hair is left on—stretched out to dry. Men and horses, dogs and boys, women drawing water or carrying wood, jostled each other. There was a glow of firelight from many a parchment window, and here and there the sound of a fiddle, scraped by some rough hunter's hand, and the quick thud of the jovial hunter's heel upon the earthen floor.

It resembled nothing in the old world so much as an Irish fair, with its shouts of laughter and snatches of song, and that sense of inextricable confusion, heightened by the all too frequent fight in a most inconvenient corner. The rule of contrary found a notable example in the name bestowed upon this charming locality. A French missionary had once resided on the spot, so it was still called La Mission.

Mathurin drew up before one of the biggest of the huts, where the sounds of mirth were loudest, and the light streamed brightest on the bank of snow beside the door.

"Here we are!" he exclaimed, swinging Wilfred from the saddle to the threshold.

CHAPTER XII.

MAXICA'S WARNING.

Mathurin knocked at the door. It was on the latch. He pushed Wilfred inside; but the boy was stubborn.

"No, no, I won't go in; I'll stand outside and wait for the others," he said. "I want my dogs."

"But the little 'un's dead beat. You would not have him hurried. I am going back to meet them," laughed Mathurin, proud of the neat way in which he had slipped out of all explanation of the blow Wilfred had received, which

85

Bowkett might make awkward.

He was in the saddle and off again in a moment, leaving Wilfred standing at the half-open door.

"This is nothing but a dodge to get my dogs away from me," thought the boy, unwilling to go inside the hut without them.

"I am landed at last," he sighed, with a grateful sense of relief, as he heard Bowkett's voice in the pause of the dance. His words were received with bursts of laughter. But what was he saying?

"It all came about through the loss of the boy. There was lamentation and mourning and woe when I went back without him. The auntie would have given her eyes to find him. See my gain by the endeavour. As hope grew beautifully less, it dwindled down to 'Bring me some certain tidings of his fate, and there is nothing I can refuse you.' As luck would have it, I came across a Blackfoot wearing the very knife we stuck in the poor boy's belt before we started. I was not slow in bartering for an exchange; and when I ride next to Acland's Hut, it is but to change horses and prepare for a longer drive to the nearest church. So, friends, I invite you all to dance at my wedding feast. Less than three days of it won't content a hunter."

A cheer went up from the noisy dancers, already calling for the fiddles.

Bowkett paused with the bow upraised. There stood Wilfred, like the skeleton at the feast, in the open doorway before him.

"If you have not found me, I have found you, Mr. Bowkett," he was saying. "I am the lost boy. I am Wilfred Acland."

The dark brow of the handsome young hunter contracted with angry dismay.

"Begone!" he exclaimed, with a toss of his head. "You! I know nothing of you! What business have you here?"

Hugh Bowkett turned his back upon Wilfred, and fiddled away more noisily than before. Two or three of his friends who stood nearest to him —men whom it would not have been pleasant to meet alone in the darkness of the night—closed round him as the dance began.

"A coyote in your lamb's-skin," laughed one, "on the lookout for a supper."

A coyote is a little wolfish creature, a most impudent thief, for ever prowling round the winter camps, nibbling at the skins and watching the meat-stage, fought off by the dogs and trapped like a rat by the hunters.

Wilfred looked round for Diomé. He might have recognized him; but no Diomé was there.

Was there not one among the merry fellows tripping before him, not one that had ever seen him before? He knew he was sadly changed. His face was still swollen from the disfiguring blow. Could he wonder if Bowkett did not know him? Should he run back and call the men who had brought him to his assistance? He hated them, every one. He was writhing still under every lash which had fallen on poor Kusky's sides. Turn to them? no, never! His dogs would be taken as payment for any help that they might give. He would reason it out. He would convince Bowkett he was the same boy.

Three or four Indians entered behind him, and seated themselves on the floor, waiting for something to eat. He knew their silent way of begging for food when they thought that food was plentiful in the camp: the high-piled meat-stage had drawn them. It was such an ordinary thing Wilfred paid no heed to them. He was bent on making Bowkett listen; and yet he was afraid to leave the door, for fear of missing his dogs.

"A word in your ear," said the most ill-looking of the hunters standing by Bowkett's fiddle, trusting to the noise of the music to drown his words from every one but him for whom they were intended. "You and I have been over the border together, sharpened up a bit among the Yankee bowie-knives. You are counting Caleb Acland as a dead man. You are expecting, as his sister's husband, to step into his shoes. Back comes this boy and sweeps the stakes out of your very hand. He'll stand first."

"I know it," retorted Bowkett with a scowl. "But," he added hurriedly, "it is not he."

"Oh, it isn't the boy you lost? Of course not. But take my advice, turn this impudent young coyote out into the snow. One midnight's frost will save you from any more bother. There are plenty of badger holes where he can rest safe and snug till doomsday."

Bowkett would not venture a reply. The low aside was unnoticed by the dancers; not the faintest breath could reach Wilfred, vainly endeavouring to pass between the whirling groups to Bowkett's side; but every syllable was caught by the quick ear of one of the Indians on the floor.

He picked up a tiny splinter of wood from the hearth, near which he was sitting; another was secreted. There were three in the hollow of his hand. Noiselessly and unobtrusively he stole behind the dancers. A gentle pull at Wilfred's coat made him look up into the half-blind eyes of Maxica the Cree.

Not a word was said. Maxica turned from him and seated himself once more on the ground, in which he deliberately stuck his three pegs.

Wilfred could not make out what he was going to do, but his heart felt lighter at the sight of him; "for," he thought, "he will confirm my story. He will tell Bowkett how he found me by the banks of the dried-up river." He dropped on the floor beside the wandering Cree. But the Indian laid a finger on his lips, and one of his pegs was pressed on Wilfred's palm; another was pointed towards Bowkett. The third, which was a little charred, and therefore blackened, was turned to the door, which Wilfred had left open, to the darkness without, from whence, according to Indian belief, the evil spirits come.

Then Maxica took the three pegs and moved them rapidly about the floor. The black peg and Bowkett's peg were always close together, rubbing against each other until both were as black as a piece of charcoal. It was clear they were pursuing the other peg—which Wilfred took for himself—from corner to corner. At last it was knocked down under them, driven right into the earthen floor, and the two blackened pegs were left sticking upright over it.

Wilfred laid his hand softly on Maxica's knee, to show his warning was understood.

But what then?

Maxica got up and glided out of the hut as noiselessly as he had entered it. The black-browed hunter whispering at Bowkett's elbow made his way through the dancers towards Wilfred with a menacing air.

"What are you doing here?" he demanded.

"Waiting to speak to Mr. Bowkett," replied Wilfred stoutly.

"Then you may wait for him on the snow-bank," retorted the hunter, seizing Wilfred by the collar and flinging him out of the door.

"What is that for?" asked several of the dancers.

"I'll vow it is the same young imp who passed us with a party of miners coming from a summer's work in the Rocky Mountains, who stole my dinner from the spit," he went on, working himself into the semblance of a passion. "I marked him with a rare black eye before we parted then, and I'll give him another if he shows his face again where I am."

"It is false!" cried Wilfred, rising up in the heat of his indignation.

His tormentor came a step or two from the door, and gathering up a great lump of snow, hurled it at him.

Wilfred escaped from the avalanche, and the mocking laughter which accompanied it, to the sheltering darkness. He paused among the sombre shadows thrown by the wall of the opposite hut. Maxica was waiting for him under its pine-bark eaves, surveying the cloudless heavens.

"He speaks with a forked tongue," said the Cree, pointing to the man in the doorway, and dividing his fingers, to show that thoughts went one way and words another.

The scorn of the savage beside him was balm to Wilfred. The touch of sympathy which makes the whole world kin drew them together. But between him and the hunter swaggering on the snow-bank there was a moral gulf nothing could bridge over. There was a sense—a strange sense —of deliverance. What would it have been to live on with such men, touching their pitch, and feeling himself becoming blackened? That was the uttermost depth from which this fellow's mistake had saved him.

It was no mistake, as Maxica was quick to show him, but deliberate purpose. Then Wilfred gave up every hope of getting back to his home. All was lost to him—even his dogs were gone.

He tried to persuade Maxica to walk round the huts with him, to find out where they were. But the Cree was resolute to get him away as fast as he could beyond the reach of Bowkett and his companions. He expected that great lump of snow would be followed by a stone; that their steps would be dogged until they reached the open, when—he did not particularize the precise form that when was likeliest to assume. The experiences of his wild, wandering life suggested dangers that could not occur to Wilfred. There must be no boyish footprint in the snow to tell which way they were going. Maxica wrapped his blanket round Wilfred, and threw him over his shoulder as if he had been a heavy pack of skins, and took his way through the noisiest part of the camp, choosing the route a frightened boy would be the last to take. He crossed in front of an outlying hut. Yula was tied by a strip of leather to one of the posts supporting its meat-stage, and Kusky to another. Maxica recognized Yula's bark before Wilfred did. He muffled the boy's head in the blanket, and drew it under his arm in such a position that Wilfred could scarcely either speak or hear. Then Maxica turned his course, and left the dogs behind him. But Yula could not be deceived. He bounded forward to the uttermost length of his tether. One sniff at the toe of Wilfred's boot, scarcely visible beneath the blanket, made him desperate. He hung at his collar; he tore up the earth; he dragged at the post, as if, like another Samson, he would use his unusual strength to pull down this prison-house.

Maxica, with his long, ungainly Indian stride, was quickly out of sight. Then Yula forbore his wailing howl, and set himself to the tough task of biting through the leathern thong which secured him. Fortunately for him, a dog-chain was unattainable in the hunters' camp. Time and persistency were safe to set him free before the daylight.

"I thought you were going to stifle me outright," said Wilfred, when Maxica released him.

"I kept you still," returned the Cree. "There were ears behind every log."

"Where are we going?" asked Wilfred.

But Maxica had no answer to that question. He was stealing over the snow with no more definite purpose before him than to take the boy away somewhere beyond the hunters' reach. A long night walk was nothing to him. He could find his way as well in the dark as in the light.

They were miles from the hunters' camp before he set Wilfred on his feet or paused to rest.

"You have saved me, Maxica," said Wilfred, in a low, deep voice. "You have saved my life from a greater danger than the snowdrift. I can only pray the Good Spirit to reward you."

"I was hunger-bitten, and you gave me beaver-skin," returned Maxica. "Now think; whilst this bad hunter keeps the gate of your house there is no going back for you, and you have neither trap nor bow. I'll guide you where the hunter will never follow—across the river to the pathless forest; and then—" he looked inquiringly, turning his dim eyes towards the boy.

"Oh, if I were but back in Hungry Hall!" Wilfred broke forth.

Maxica was leading on to where a poplar thicket concealed the entrance to a sheltered hollow scooped on the margin of a frozen stream. The snow had fallen from its shelving sides, and lay in white masses, blocking the entrance from the river. Giving Wilfred his hand, Maxica began to descend the slippery steep. It was one of nature's hiding-places, which Maxica had frequently visited. He scooped out his circle in the frozen snow at the bottom, fetched down the dead wood from the overhanging trees, and built his fire, as on the first night of their acquaintance. But now the icy walls around them reflected the dancing flames in a thousand varied hues. Between the black rocks, from which the raging winds had swept the recent snow, a cascade turned to ice hung like a drapery of crystal lace suspended in mid-air.

It was the second night they had passed together, with no curtain but the star-lit sky. Now Maxica threw the corner of his blanket over Wilfred's shoulders, and drew him as closely to his side as if he were his son. The Cree lit his pipe, and abandoned himself to an hour or two of pure Indian enjoyment.

Wilfred nestled by his side, thinking of Jacob on his stony pillow. The rainbow flashes from the frozen fall gleamed before him like stairs of light, by which God's messengers could come and go. It is at such moments, when we lie powerless in the grasp of a crushing danger, and sudden help appears in undreamed-of ways, that we know a mightier power than man's is caring for us.

He thought of his father and mother—the love he had missed and mourned; and love was springing up for him again in stranger hearts, born of the pity for his great trouble.

There was a patter on the snow. It was not the step of a man. With a soft and stealthy movement Maxica grasped his bow, and was drawing the arrow from his quiver, when Yula bounded into Wilfred's arms. There was a piteous whine from the midst of the poplars, where Kusky stood shivering, afraid to follow. To scramble up by the light of the fire and bring him down was the work of a moment.

Yula's collar was still round his neck, with the torn thong dangling from it; but Kusky had slipped his head out of his, only leaving a little of his abundant hair behind him.

Three hours' rest sufficed for Maxica. He rose and shook himself.

"That other place," he said, "where's that?"

Now his dogs were with him, Wilfred was loath to leave their icy retreat and face the cruel world.

The fireshine and the ice, with all their mysterious beauty, held him spellbound.

"Maxica," he whispered, not understanding the Cree's last question, "they call this the new world; but don't you think it really is the very old, old world, just as God made it? No one has touched it in all these ages."

Yes, it was a favourite nook of Maxica's, beautiful, he thought, as the happy hunting-grounds beyond the sunset—the Indian's heaven. Could he exchange the free range of his native wilds, with all their majestic beauty, for a settler's hut? the trap and the bow for the plough and the spade, and tie himself down to one small corner? The earth was free to all. Wilfred had but to take his share, and roam its plains and forests, as the red man roamed.

But Wilfred knew better than to think he could really live their savage life, with its dark alternations of hunger and cold.

"Could I get back to Hungry Hall in time to travel with Mr. De Brunier?" he asked his swarthy friend.

"Yes; that other place," repeated Maxica, "where is that?"

Wilfred could hardly tell him, he remembered so little of the road.

"Which way did the wind blow and the snow drift past as you stood at the friendly gates?" asked Maxica. "On which cheek did the wind cut keenest when you rode into the hunters' camp at nightfall?"

Wilfred tried to recollect.

"A two days' journey," reflected Maxica, "with the storm-wind in our faces."

He felt the edge of his hatchet, climbed the steep ascent, and struck a gash in the stem of the nearest poplar. His quick sense of touch told him at which edge of the cut the bark grew thickest. That was the north. He found it with the unerring precision of the mariner's compass. Although he had no names for the cardinal points, he knew them all.

There was an hour or two yet before daylight. Wilfred found himself a stick, as they passed between the poplars, to help himself along, and caught up Kusky under his other arm; for the poor little fellow was stiff in every limb, and his feet were pricked and bleeding, from the icicles which he had suffered to gather between his toes, not yet knowing any better. But he was too big a dog for Wilfred to carry long. Wilfred carefully broke out the crimsoned spikes as soon as there was light enough to show him what was the matter, and Yula came and washed Kusky's feet more than once; so they helped him on.

Before the gray of the winter's dawn La Mission was miles behind them, and breakfast a growing necessity.

Maxica had struck out a new route for himself. He would not follow the track Batiste and his companions had taken. The black pegs might yet pursue the white and trample it down in the snow if they were not wary. Sooner or later an Indian accomplishes his purpose. He attributed the same fierce determination to Bowkett. Wilfred lagged more and more. Food must be had. Maxica left him to contrive a trap in the run of the game through the bushes to their right. So Wilfred took the dogs slowly on. Sitting down in the snow, without first clearing a hole or lighting a fire, was dangerous.

Yula, sharing in the general desire for breakfast, started off on a little hunting expedition of his own. Kusky was limping painfully after him, as he darted between the tall, dark pines which began to chequer the landscape and warn the travellers they were nearing the river.

Wilfred went after his dog to recall him. The sun was glinting through the trees, and the all-pervading stillness was broken by the sound of a hatchet. Had Maxica crossed over unawares? Had Wilfred turned back without knowing it? He drew to the spot. There was Diomé chopping firewood, which Pe-na-Koam was dragging across the snow towards a roughly-built log-hut.

She dropped the boughs on the snow, and drawing her blanket round her, came to meet him.

Diomé, not perceiving Wilfred's approach, had retreated further among the trees, intent upon his occupation.

Wilfred's first sensation of joy at the sight of Pe-na-Koam turned to something like fear as he saw her companion, for he had known him only as Bowkett's man. But retreat was impossible. The old squaw had shuffled up to him and grasped his arm. The sight of Yula bounding over the snow had made her the first to perceive him. She was pouring forth her delight in her Indian tongue, and explaining her appearance in such altered surroundings. Wilfred could not understand a word, but Maxica was not far behind. Kusky and Yula were already in the hut, barking for the wa-wa (the goose) that was roasting before the fire.

93

When Maxica came up, walking beside Diomé, Wilfred knew escape was out of the question. He must try to make a friend—at least he must meet him as a friend, even if he proved himself to be an enemy. But the work was done already.

"Ah, it is you!" cried Diomé. "I was sure it was. You had dropped a button in the tumble-down hut, and the print of your boot, an English boot, was all over the snow when I got there. You look dazed, my little man; don't you understand what I'm talking about? That old squaw is my grandmother. You don't know, of course, who it was sent the Blackfoot Sapoo to dig her out of the snow; but I happen to know. The old man is going from Hungry Hall, and Louison is to be promoted. I'm on the look-out to take his place with the new-comer; so when I met with him, a snow-bird whispered in my ear a thing or two. But where are your guides?"

Wilfred turned for a word with Maxica before he dared reply.

Both felt the only thing before them was to win Diomé to Wilfred's side.

"Have you parted company with Bowkett?" asked Maxica cautiously.

"Bowkett," answered Diomé, "is going to marry and turn farmer, and I to try my luck as voyageur to the Company. This is the hunters' idle month, and I am waiting here until my services are wanted at the fort.—What cheer?" he shouted to his bright-eyed little wife, driving the dogs from the door of the hut.

The wa-wa shortly disappeared before Maxica's knife, for an Indian likes about ten pounds of meat for a single meal. Wilfred was asleep beside the fire long before it was over; when they tried to rouse him his senses were roaming. The excitement and exertion, following the blow on his head, had taken effect at last.

Pe-na-Koam, with all an Indian woman's skill in the use of medicinal herbs, and the experience of a long life spent among her warrior tribe, knew well how to take care of him.

"Leave him to me," she said to Maxica, "and go your ways."

Diomé too was anxious for the Cree to depart. He was looking forward to taking Wilfred back to Acland's Hut himself. Caleb Acland's gratitude would express itself in a tangible form, and he did not intend to divide it with Maxica. His evident desire to get rid of the Cree put the red man on his guard. Long did he sit beside the hunter's fire in brooding silence, trusting that Wilfred might rise up from his lengthened sleep ready to travel, as an Indian might have done. But his hope was abortive. He drew out of Pe-na-Koam all he wanted to know. Diomé had been long in Bowkett's employ. When the Cree heard this he shut his lips.

"Watch over the boy," he said to Pe-na-Koam, "for danger threatens him."

Then Maxica went out and set his traps in the fir-brake and the marsh, keeping stealthy watch round the hut for fear Bowkett should appear, and often looking in to note Wilfred's progress.

One day the casual mention of Bowkett's name threw the poor boy into such a state of agitation, Diomé suspected there had been some passage between the two he was ignorant of. A question now and then, before Wilfred was himself again, convinced him the boy had been to La Mission, and that Bowkett had refused to recognize him. When he spoke of it to Pe-na-Koam, she thought of the danger at which Maxica had hinted. She watched for the Cree. Diomé began to fear Wilfred's reappearance might involve him in a quarrel with Bowkett.

As Wilfred got better, and found Hungry Hall was shut up, he resolved to go back to Acland's Hut, if possible, whilst his Aunt Miriam and Bowkett were safe out of the way on their road to the church where they were to be married. Diomé said they would be gone two days. He proposed to take Wilfred with him, when he went to the wedding, on the return of the bride and bridegroom.

"Lend me your snow-shoes," entreated Wilfred, "and with Maxica for a guide, I can manage the journey alone. Don't go with me, Diomé, for Bowkett will never forgive the man who takes me back. You have been good and kind to me, why should I bring you into trouble?"

CHAPTER XIII.

JUST IN TIME.

The walk from Diomé's log hut to Uncle Caleb's farm was a long one, but the clear, bright sunshine of December had succeeded the pitiless sleet and blinding snow. Lake and river had hardened in the icy breath of the north wind. An iron frost held universal sway, as Wilfred and Maxica drew near to Acland's Hut.

95

The walk to Uncle Caleb's farm was a long one.

The tinkle of a distant sledge-bell arrested Maxica. Had some miscount in the day brought them face to face with the bridal party?

They turned away from the well-known gate, crept behind the farm buildings, and crossed the reedy pool to Forgill's hut.

With the frozen snow full three feet deep beneath their feet there was roadway everywhere. Railings scarcely showed above it, and walls could be easily cleared with one long step. The door of the hut was fastened, but Wilfred waited behind it while Maxica stole round to reconnoitre.

He returned quickly. It was not the bridal party, for there was not a single squaw among them. They were travellers in a horse-sledge, stopping at the farm to rest. He urged Wilfred to seize the chance and enter with them. The presence of the strangers would be a protection. They took their way through the orchard trees, and came out boldly on the well-worn tracks before the gate. It excited no surprise in the occupants of the sledge to see two dusky figures in their long, pointed snow-shoes gliding swiftly after them; travellers like themselves, no doubt, hoping to find hospitality at the farm.

Yula and Kusky went bounding over the intervening space.

There were two travellers and a sledge-driver. The dogs considered them, and did not bark. Then Kusky, in frantic delight, endeavoured to leap into the sledge. It drew up. The driver thundered on the gate.

"What cheer?" shouted a voice from the sledge.

It was the usual traveller's inquiry, but it thrilled through Wilfred's ears, for it was—it could not be—yet it was the voice of Mr. De Brunier.

Kusky was already on Gaspé's knee devouring him with his doggie caresses.

"Is it a dream, or is it real?" asked Wilfred, as with one long slide he overtook the sledge, and grasped a hand of each.

"I didn't know you, coming after us in your seven-league boots," laughed Gaspé, pointing to the long, oval frame of Wilfred's snow-shoes, reaching a foot or more before and behind his boot.

But Wilfred did not answer, he was whispering rapidly to Mr. De Brunier.

"Wilfred, *mon ami,*" (my friend), pursued Gaspé, bent upon interrupting the low-voiced confidence, "it was for your sake grandfather decided to make his first inquiries for a farm in this neighbourhood. Batiste was so ambiguous and so loath to speak of your journey when he came after Louison's post, we grew uneasy about you. All the more glad to find you safe at home."

"At home, but not in home," answered Wilfred, significantly laying his finger on his lips, to prevent any exclamation from his bewildered friend.

"All right," said Mr. De Brunier. "We will enter together."

Pête, who was already opening the gate, bade them heartily welcome. Hospitality in the lone North-West becomes a duty.

Wilfred dropped behind the sledge, slouched his fur cap well over his eyes, and let Maxica fold his blanket round him, Indian fashion.

Pête led the way into the kitchen, Wilfred followed behind the sledge-driver, and the Cree was the last to enter. A long row of joints were roasting before the ample fire, giving undoubted indications of an approaching feast.

"Just in time," observed Mr. De Brunier with a smile, which gained a peculiar significance as it rested on Wilfred.

"Ay, and that you are," returned old Pête; "for the missis is gone to be married, and I was on the look-out for her return when I heard the jingling of your sledge-bells. The house will be full enough by nightfall, I reckon."

Wilfred undid the strap of his snow-shoes, gave them to Maxica, and walked softly to the door of his uncle's room.

97

He opened it with a noiseless hand, and closed it behind him.

Mr. De Brunier's retort about the welcome which awaited uninvited guests on a bridal night kept Pête from noticing his movements.

The logs crackled and the sparks flew on the kitchen hearth. The fat from the savoury roast fell hissing in the pan, and the hungry travellers around it seemed to have eyes for nothing else.

Wilfred crept to his uncle's bed. He was asleep. The boy glanced round. He threw off his wraps. His first care was to find his uncle's comb and brush. It was a luxury unknown since his departure from Hungry Hall. He was giving a good tug at his tangled locks, hoping to make himself look a little more like the schoolboy who had once before roused the old man from his sleep, when a cough and an exclamation sounding like, "Who is there?" told him his uncle was awake.

"O uncle, you surely have not forgotten me—me, your nephew, Wilfred! Got home at last. The pony threw me, and I was utterly lost. An Indian guided me here," he answered, tumbling his words one upon another as fast as he could, for his heart was beating wildly.

Caleb Acland raised himself on one elbow and grasped Wilfred by the wrist. "It is he! It is flesh and blood!" he ejaculated. "The boy himself Pête! Pête!" He felt for the stick left leaning against his bed, and stamped it on the floor.

A great sob burst unawares from the poor boy's lips.

"Don't!" said the old man in alarm. "What are you crying for, lad? What's happened? I don't understand. Give me your hand! That's cold enough— death cold. Pête! Pête! what are ye about? Have you grown deaf that you can't hear me?"

He pulled Wilfred's cold fingers under the blankets and tried to chafe them between his swollen hands.

"I'm not crying," protested Wilfred, brushing his other hand across his eyes. "It is the ice melting out of me. I'm thawing all over. It is because I have got back uncle, and you are glad to have me. I should have been dead but for the Cree who brought me home. I was almost starving at times. I have wandered in the snow all night."

"God bless the boy!" ejaculated the old man, thundering on the floor once more.

"Here, Pête! Pête! Something quick to eat."

Pête's head appeared at the door at last.

"Whatever do you want now, master?" he demanded in an injured tone. "I thought I had put everything ready for you, as handy as could be; and you said you wouldn't call me off, with the bride expected every minute, and the supper to cook, as you know."

"Cook away then," returned his master impatiently. "It is the hour for the fatted calf. Oh, you've no eyes, none! Whom have I got here? Who is this?"

Pête backed to the door in wide-eyed wonder. "I'm struck of a heap!" he gasped, staring at Wilfred as if he thought he would melt away into vacancy.

"Where were you that you did not see him come in?" asked his master sharply.

"Where?" repeated Pête indignantly. "At your own gate, answering a party of travellers—men who've come down to buy land; and," he added, changing his tone, "there is a gentleman among them says he must speak to you, master, your own self particular, this very night."

"It is Mr. De Brunier, uncle. He took me in, and sent me to the hunters' camp, where Mr. Bowkett was to be found," interposed Wilfred.

This name was spoken with an effort. Like many a noble-minded boy, Wilfred hated to tell of another. He hesitated, then went on abruptly: "I thought he would be sure to bring me home. Well, I got there. He did not seem to know me. He was all for fiddling and dancing. They were a rough set, uncle, a very rough set. Father would not have liked to have seen me with such men. I got away again as quickly as I could. The Cree who had saved me before guided me home at last."

"What is that? Did you say Bowkett, Hugh Bowkett?" repeated the old man. "Why, your aunt was married to him this morning."

When Pête disappeared into his master's room, Maxica, who had seated himself on the kitchen floor, rose suddenly, and leaning over Mr. De Brunier, asked, "Who in this place is friend to the boy without a father?"

"I can answer your question for myself, but no further, for I am a stranger here," replied Mr. De Brunier.

"We are four," said Maxica, counting on his fingers. "I hear the voice of the man at the gate—the man who spoke against the white boy with a forked tongue; the man who drove him out into the frosty night, that it might kill him. We have brought the marten to the trap. If it closes on him, Maxica stays to break it."

"Come outside, where we can talk freely," answered Mr. De Brunier, leading the way.

Gaspé and the sledge-driver were left to the enjoyment of the roaring fire. They were considering the state of Kusky's feet. Gaspé was removing the icicles from his toes, and the man of the sledge was warmly recommending boots, and describing the way to make them, when the shouts at the gate told them the bridal party had arrived. The stupid Pête, as they began to think, had vanished, for no one answered the summons. Gaspé guessed the reason, and sent the man to open the gate. He silenced the dogs, and drew back into the corner, with instinctive good breeding, to make himself as little in the way as possible.

The great farm-house kitchen was entrance-hall as well. Every door opened into it. On one hand was the dining-room, reserved chiefly for state occasions; on the other, the storeroom. The family sleeping rooms were at the back. Like a provident housewife, Aunt Miriam had set the tables for her marriage feast, and filled the storeroom with good things, before she went to church. Pête, with a Frenchman's genius for the spit, could manage the rest.

The arrival of one or two other guests at the same moment detained the bridal party with their noisy greetings.

When Aunt Miriam entered the kitchen, leaning on her bridegroom's arm, Gaspé was almost asleep in his dim corner.

Out ran Pête, effervescing with congratulations, and crossing the heartiness of the bridal welcome with the startling exclamation, "The boy, Mrs. Bowkett!—the boy's come home!"

The bridegroom looked sharply round. "The boy," he repeated, seeing Gaspé by the fire. "There he is."

Up sprang Gaspé, bowing to the bride with all the courtly grace of the chivalrous De Bruniers of Breton days.

Aunt Miriam turned her head away. "O Pête!" she groaned, "I thought—I thought you meant—"

Bowkett did not let her finish her sentence, he hurried her into the dining-

100

room. Behind him came his bright-eyed sister, who had played the part of bridesmaid, and was eager for the dancing and the fun, so soon to commence. At her side walked Forgill in his Sunday best, all important with the responsibility of his position, acting as proxy for his old master. He had given the bride away, and was at that moment cogitating over some half-dozen sentences destined for the after-dinner speech which he knew would be required of him. They were restive, and would not follow each other. "Happy day" and "Best wishes" wanted setting up on stilts, with a few long words to back them, for such an occasion. He knew the Indian love of speechifying would be too strong in their hunter guests to let him off. He had got as far as, "Uncommonly happy day for us all." But "uncommonly" sounded far too common in his critical ears. He was searching for a finer-sounding word, and thought he had got it in "preternaturally," when he heard the feeble voice of his master calling out, "Miriam! Here, Miriam."

"Are they all deaf?" said Caleb Acland to Wilfred. "Open the door, my lad, and show yourself to your aunt."

Slowly and reluctantly Wilfred obeyed him. He held it open just a hand-breadth, and met the scowling brow of the owner of the forked tongue.

There was mutual recognition in the glance exchanged.

Wilfred shut the door softly, and drew the bolt without attracting his uncle's attention.

"The place is full of strangers," he said; "I shall see auntie soon. I'd rather wait here with you. I shall be sure to see her before she goes to her new home."

"As you like, my boy;—that Pête's a cow. There is no going away to a new home. It is bringing in a new master here before the old one is gone, so that your aunt should not be left unprotected a single day."

As Caleb Acland spoke, Wilfred felt himself growing hard and desperate in the cold clutch of a giant despair. The star of hope dropped from his sky. He saw himself in the hand of the man who had turned him from his door into the killing frost.

It was too late to speak out; Bowkett would be sure to deny it, and hate him the more. No, not a word to Uncle Caleb until he had taken counsel with Mr. De Brunier. But in his hasty glance into the outer world Mr. De Brunier was nowhere to be seen.

101

Wilfred was sure he would not go away without seeing him again. There was nothing for it but to gain a little time, wait with his uncle until the wedding guests were shut in the dining-room, and then go out and find Mr. De Brunier, unless Aunt Miriam had invited him to sit down with them. Yes, she was sure to do that, and Gaspé would be with his grandfather. But Maxica was there. He had saved him twice. He knew what Maxica would say: "To the free wild forest, and learn the use of the trap and the bow with me."

Wilfred was sorely tempted to run away. The recollection of Mr. De Brunier's old-world stories restrained him. He thought of the Breton emigrants. "What did they do in their despair? What all men can do, their duty." He kept on saying these words over and over, asking himself, "What is my duty? Have I no duty to the helpless old man who has welcomed me so kindly? How will Bowkett behave to him?" Wilfred felt much stronger to battle through with the hunter on his uncle's behalf, than when he thought only of himself. "The brave and loyal die at their posts. Gaspé would, rather than run away—rather than do anything that looked like running away."

"What is the matter with you, Wilfred?" asked his uncle anxiously. "What makes you stand like that, my boy?"

"I am so tired," answered Wilfred, "I have walked all day to-day, and all day yesterday. If I take the cushion out of your chair for a pillow, I might lie down before the stove, uncle."

"That Pête is an ass not to bring something to eat, as if he could not make those fellows in the dining-room wait half-a-minute. But stop, there is some broth keeping hot on the stove. Take that, and come and lie down on the bed by me; then I can see you and feel you, and know I have got you again," answered Uncle Caleb, as if he had some presentiment of what was passing in Wilfred's mind.

Glad enough to obey, Wilfred drank the broth eagerly, and came to the bed. The old man took him by both hands and gazed in his face, murmuring, "Lord, now lettest thou thy servant depart in peace."

The peace that Uncle Caleb rejoiced in was his own alone; all around him strife was brewing. But his peace was of that kind which circumstances cannot give or take away.

"Kneel down beside me just one minute, my boy," he went on. "We must not be like the nine lepers, who forgot the thanks when the good had

102

come. They wouldn't even with the tailors, for in the whole nine put together there was not one bit of a true man, or they could not have done it."

Wilfred fell on his knees and repeated softly the Christ-taught prayer of the ages, "Our Father who art in heaven." He remembered how he had been fed from the wild bird's *cache*, and saved by the wild man's pity, and his heart was swelling. But when he came to "Forgive us our trespasses, as we forgive them that trespass against us," he stopped abruptly.

"Go on," whispered the old man softly.

"I can't," muttered Wilfred. "It isn't in my heart; I daren't go on. It is speaking with a forked tongue: words one way, thoughts another; telling lies to God."

Caleb Acland looked at him as if he were slowly grasping the position.

"Is it Bowkett that you can't forgive?" he asked gently. "Did you think he need not have lost you? Did you think he would not know you, my poor boy?"

"Have I got to live with him always?" returned Wilfred.

"No, not if you don't like him. I'll send you back to school," answered his uncle in a tone of decision.

"Do you mean it, uncle? Do you really say that I shall go back to school?" exclaimed the boy, his heavy heart's lead beginning to melt, as the way of escape opened so unexpectedly before him.

"It is a promise," repeated the old man soothingly. It was obvious now there was something wrong, which the boy refused to explain.

"Patience a bit," he thought; "I can't distress him. It will leak out soon; but it is growing strange that nobody comes near us."

CHAPTER XIV

WEDDING GUESTS.

More guests were arriving—Diomé, Batiste, Mathurin, and a dozen others. Bowkett came out into the porch to receive them, and usher one after the other into the dining-room. As the last went in before him, his friend Dick Vanner of the forked tongue tapped him on the shoulder.

"Who is in there?" he whispered. "Did you see?" pointing as he spoke to the door of Uncle Caleb's room.

103

Gaspé was on the alert in a moment, longing to break a lance in his friend's behalf. The men dropped their voices, but the echo of one sentence reached him. It sounded like, "No, she only saw the other boy."

"So, Wilfred, *mon cher,* you and I have changed places, and I have become that 'other boy,'" laughed Gaspé to himself, lying perdu with an open ear.

As the two separated they muttered, "Outwit us? Like to see it done!"

"Keep that door shut, and leave the rest to me," added Vanner, sauntering up to the fire.—"Accommodation is scanty here to-night. How many are there in your party?" he asked, looking down on Gaspé. "Pête said four—three men and a boy. Was not it five—three men and two boys?"

"Yes, five," answered Gaspé.

"You boys must want something to eat," remarked Vanner, carelessly pushing open the door of the storeroom, and returning with a partridge pie. "Here, fall to. Where's your chum?"

Gaspé saw the trap into which he was expected to walk. He stepped over it.

"Have not you been taught to look out for number one?" asked Gaspé. "I'll have a turn at that pie by myself, now I have got the chance, before I call on a chum to help me. I can tell you that."

"Confound you, you greedy young beggar!" exclaimed Vanner.

"Try thirty miles in an open sled, with twenty-five degrees of frost on the ground, and see if you would be willing to divide your pie at the end of it," retorted Gaspé.

"That is a cool way of asking for one apiece," remarked Vanner, abstracting a second pie from the storeroom shelves.

"If you've another to spare I'd like two for myself," persisted Gaspé.

"Then have it," said Vanner. "I am bound to give you a satisfaction. We do not reckon on a wedding feast every night. Now, where is the other boy? You can't object to call him. Here is a sausage as long as your arm. Walk into that."

"You will not get me to move with this dish before me," returned the undaunted Gaspé, and Vanner felt it waste of time to urge him further. He went back to his friends.

Gaspé was at Caleb Acland's door in a moment, singing through the keyhole,—

> "St. George he is for England, St. Denis is for France.
> *Honi soit qui mal y pense.*"

Wilfred rose to open the door as he recognized his friend's voice.

"Keep where you are. Don't come out for anybody," urged Gaspé, retreating as he heard a noise: but it was only his grandfather re-entering the porch.

He flew to his side. "What's up?" he asked breathlessly.

"A goodly crop of suspicions, if all the Cree tells me is true. Your poor friend is fitted with an uncle in this Bowkett after their old ballad type of the Babes in the Wood."

"Now listen to me, grandfather, and I can tell you a little bit more," answered Gaspé, giving his narrative with infinite delight at the success of his manoeuvring.

The moon shone clear and bright. The tree in the centre of the court, laden with hoar-frost, glittered in its crystal white like some bridal bouquet of gigantic size. The house was ablaze with light from every window. The hunters had turned their horses adrift. They were galloping at will among the orchard trees to keep themselves warm. Maxica was wandering in their midst, counting their numbers to ascertain the size of the party. Mr. De Brunier crossed over to him, to discuss Gaspé's intelligence, and sent his grandson back indoors, where the sledge-driver was ready to assist him in the demolition of the pies which had so signally failed to lure Wilfred from his retreat.

Mr. De Brunier followed his grandson quickly, and walking straight to Uncle Caleb's door, knocked for admittance.

The cowkeeper, the only individual at Acland's Hut who did not know Wilfred personally, was sent by Bowkett to keep up the kitchen fire.

The man stared. "The master has got his door fastened," he said; "I can't make it out."

"Is Mr. Acland ready to see me?" asked Mr. De Brunier, repeating his summons.

"Yes," answered Uncle Caleb; "come in."

105

Wilfred opened the door.

Uncle Caleb raised himself on his elbow, and catching sight of the dishes on the kitchen-table, said, "It seems to me the old man's orders are to go for little. But whilst the life is in me I am master in this place. Be so good, sir, as to tell that fellow of mine to bring that pie in here, and give this child something to eat."

"With pleasure," returned his visitor.

Wilfred's supper provided for, the two looked well at each other.

"What sort are you?" was the question in both minds. They trusted, as we all do more or less, to the expression. A good honest character writes itself on the face. They shook hands.

"I have to thank you for bringing back my boy," said Uncle Caleb.

"Not me," returned Mr. De Brunier, briefly recapitulating the circumstances which led to Wilfred's sojourn at Hungry Hall, and why he sent him to the hunters' camp. "Since then," he added, "your nephew has been wandering among the Indians. It was a Cree who guided him home —the same Cree who warned him not to trust himself with Bowkett."

"Come here, Wilfred, and tell me exactly what this Indian said," interposed Caleb Acland, a grave look gathering on his wrinkled brow.

"Not one word, uncle. Maxica did not speak," answered Wilfred. "He brought me three queer bits of wood from the hearth and stuck them in the floor before me, so, and so," continued the boy, trying to explain the way in which the warning had been given to him.

Uncle Caleb was getting so much exhausted with the excitement of Wilfred's return, and the effort of talking to a stranger, he did not quite understand all Wilfred was saying.

"We can't condemn a fellow on evidence like that," moaned the old man, "and one so near to me as Bowkett. What does it mean for Miriam?"

"Will you see this Cree and hear for yourself?" asked Mr. De Brunier. "We are neither judge nor jury. We are not here to acquit or condemn, but a warning like this is not to be despised. I came to put you on your guard."

The feeble hand grasped his, "I am about spent," groaned Caleb. "It is my breath. Let me rest a bit. I'll think this over. Come again."

The gasping words came with such painful effort, Mr. De Brunier could only lay him back amongst his pillows and promise to return in the morning, or earlier if it were wished. He was at the door, when Caleb Acland signed to him to return.

"Not a word to my sister yet. The boy is safe here. Tell him he is not to go out of this room."

Mr. De Brunier shook the feeble hand once more, and gave the required promise. There was one more word. "What was that about buying land? I might help you there; a little business between us, you understand."

"Yes, yes," answered Mr. De Brunier, feeling as if such another effort might shake the labouring breath out of the enfeebled frame in a moment.

"Keep in here. Keep quiet; and remember, whatever happens, I shall be near," was Mr. De Brunier's parting charge to Wilfred as he went back into the kitchen, intending to watch there through the night, if no one objected to his presence.

The old man started as the door closed after him. "Don't fasten it, lad!" he exclaimed. "It looks too much like being afraid of them."

Mr. De Brunier joined Gaspé and the sledge-driver at their supper. Gaspé watched him attentively as they ate on in silence.

Bowkett came out and spoke to them. "I am sorry," he said, "to seem inhospitable, but the house is so full to-night I really cannot offer you any further accommodation. But the men have a sleeping hut round the corner, under the pines, where you can pass the night. I'll send one of them with you to show you the way and light a fire."

No exception could be taken to this. The three finished their supper and were soon ready to depart.

"I must see Mr. Acland again about the land business," remarked Mr. De Brunier, recalling Uncle Caleb's hint.

Bowkett summoned his man, and Diomé came out with him. He strolled through the porch and looked about him, as if he were considering the weather.

Maxica was still prowling behind the orchard trees, like a hungry coyote watching for the remnants of the feast, as it seemed. The two met.

"There will be mischief before these fellows part," said Diomé. "Keep a sharp look-out for the boy."

107

Diomé went on to catch Dick Vanner's pony. Maxica stole up to the house. The travellers were just coming out. He gave Yula a call. Gaspé was the only one who perceived him, as Yula bounded between them.

It was hard for Gaspé to go away and leave his friend without another word. He had half a mind to take Kusky with him. He lingered irresolute a moment or two behind his grandfather. Bowkett had opened the door of Caleb Acland's room, and he saw Kusky creeping in between Bowkett's legs.

"How is this?" the latter was saying in a noisy voice. "Wilfred got home, and won't show his face!—won't come out amongst us to have his dinner and speak to his aunt! What is the meaning of it? What makes him afraid of being seen?"

There was not a word from Wilfred. It was the feeble voice of his Uncle Caleb that was speaking:—

"Yes, it is Wilfred come back. I've got him here beside me all safe. He has been wandering about among the redskins, half dead and nearly starved. Don't disturb us. I am getting him to sleep. Tell Miriam she must come here and look at him. You all come and look at him; Forgill and your Diomé too. They all know my boy. How has Miriam managed to keep away?"

"As if we could spare the bride from the marriage feast," laughed Bowkett, raising his voice that every one might hear what they were saying.

"Neither can I spare my boy out of my sight a single moment," said the old man quietly.

"That's capital," laughed Gaspé to himself, as he ran after his grandfather.

They did not encounter Maxica, but they passed Diomé trying to catch the horse, and gave him a little help by the way.

"You are not going?" he asked anxiously. "I thought you would be sure to stay the night. You are a friend of Wilfred Acland's, are you not, Mr. De Brunier? He was so disappointed when he found Hungry Hall was shut up. I thought you would know him; so do I. Mrs. Bowkett says the boy is not her nephew."

"I rather think that has been said for her," remarked Mr. De Brunier quietly.

"I see through it," exclaimed Gaspé; "I see what they are driving at. Her

108

husband told her I was the boy. She came and looked at me. Bowkett knows well enough the real Wilfred is in his uncle's room, If they could get him out into the kitchen, they would make a great clamour and declare he is an impostor trying to take the old man in."

"You've hit it," muttered Diomé. "But they shan't give him lynch law. I'll not stand by and see that."

"Come back, grandfather," cried Gaspé. "Give me one of your English sovereigns with a little silver threepenny on either side to kiss it. I'll string them on my watch-chain for a lady's locket, walk in with it for a wedding present, and undeceive the bride before them all."

"Not so fast, Gaspard. We should only bring the crisis before we have raised our safeguards," rejoined Mr. De Brunier thoughtfully. "I saw many a gun set down against the wall, as the hunters came in."

"That is nothing," put in Diomé; "we are never without them."

"That is everything," persisted Mr. De Brunier. "Men with arms habitually in their hands use them with small provocation, and things are done which would never be done by deliberate purpose."

"I am not Dick Vanner's groom," said Diomé, "but he wants me to hold his horse in the shadow of those pines or under the orchard wall; and I'll hold it as long as he likes, and walk it about half the night in readiness for him, and then I shall know where he is bound for."

"The American frontier, with Wilfred behind him, unless I am making a great mistake. If Bowkett laid a finger on him here, half his guests would turn upon him," observed Mr. De Brunier.

"That's about it," returned Diomé. "Now I am going to shut up this horse in one of the sheds, ready for Vanner at a moment's notice, and then I'll try for a word with Forgill. He is working so hard with the carving-knife there is no getting at him."

"There is one of the Aclands' men lighting a fire in his hut, ready for us," put in Gaspé.

Diomé shook his head. "He!" he repeated in accents of contempt; "he would let it all out at the wrong time."

"Is the Cree gone?"

"Maxica is on the scent already,' replied Diomé, whistling carelessly as they parted.

109

"Gaspard," said Mr. De Brunier, as they entered the hut, "do you remember passing a policeman on the road. He was watching for a Yankee spirit cart, contraband of course. He will have caught it by this time, and emptied the barrels, according to our new Canadian law. Go back in the sledge—you will meet him returning—and bring him here. If he rides into the farm-court before daybreak, your little friend is safe. As for me, I must keep watch here. No one can leave the house without me seeing him, the night is so clear. A dark figure against the white ground is visible at twice this distance; and Maxica is somewhere by the back of the homestead. Neither sight nor sound will escape an Indian."

Mr. De Brunier despatched the sledge-driver back to the farm with the man Bowkett had sent to light their fire, to try to procure a fresh horse. This was easily managed. Bowkett was delighted to think the travellers were about to resume their journey, and declared the better half of hospitality was to speed the parting guest.

The sledge went round to Forgill's hut. Gaspé wrapped himself in the bearskin and departed. No one saw him go; no one knew that Mr. De Brunier was left behind. He built up the fire and reconnoitred his ground. In one corner of the hut was a good stout cudgel.

"I must anticipate your owner's permission and adopt you," he said, as he gave it a flourish to try its weight. Then he looked to the revolver in his breast pocket, and began his walk, so many paces in front of the hut, with his eye on the farm-house porch, and so many paces walking backwards, with it still in sight—a self-appointed sentry, ready to challenge the enemy single-handed, for he did not count much upon Diomé. He saw how loath he was to come into collision with Bowkett, and reckoned him more as a friend in the camp than as an active ally. There was Maxica, ready like a faithful mastiff to fly at the throat of the first man who dared to lay a hand on Wilfred, regardless of consequences. He did not know Maxica, but he knew the working of the Indian mind. Revenge is the justice of the savage. It was Maxica's retaliation that he feared. Diomé had spoken of Forgill, but Mr. De Brunier knew nothing of him, so he left him out of count. It was clear he must chiefly rely on his own coolness and courage. "The moral force will tell in such an encounter as this, and that is all on my side," he said to himself. "It will tell on the outsiders and the farm-servants. I shall find some to second me." He heard the scrape of the fiddle and the merry chorus of some hunting-song, followed by the quick beat of the dancers' footsteps.

Hour succeeded hour. The fire in the hut burned low. De Brunier left his post for a moment to throw on fresh logs. He returned to his watch. The house-door opened. Out came Diomé and crossed to the cattle-sheds. Mr. De Brunier saw him come back with Vanner's horse. He changed his position, creeping in behind the orchard trees, until he was within a few yards of the house. The three feet of snow beneath his feet gave him an elevation. He was looking down into the court, where the snow had been partially cleared.

Diomé was walking the horse up and down before the door. It was not a night in which any one could stand still. His impatient stamping to warm his feet brought out Vanner and Bowkett, with half-a-dozen others. The leave-taking was noisy and prolonged. Batiste's head appeared in the doorway.

"I cannot count on his assistance," thought Mr. De Brunier, "but I can count on his neutrality; and Diomé must know that a word from me would bring about his dismissal from his new master."

Vanner mounted and rode off along the slippery ground as only a hunter could ride.

"Now for the first act," thought Mr. De Brunier. "May my Gaspard be speeding on his errand. The hour draws near."

As Bowkett and his friends turned back into the house, Diomé walked rapidly across the other end of the orchard and went towards Forgill's hut. With cautious steps De Brunier followed.

Diomé was standing moodily by the fire. He started.

"Well," demanded Mr. De Brunier, "how goes the night?"

"For God's sake keep out of the way, sir. They have made this hut the rendezvous, believing you had started hours ago," exclaimed Diomé brightening.

"Did you think I had deserted the poor boy?" asked Mr. De Brunier.

"I was thinking," answered Diomé, waiving the question, "Dick Vanner is a dangerous fellow to thwart when the bowie-knife is in his hand."

"Well, you will see it done, and then you may find him not quite so dangerous as he seems," was the quiet reply.

111

CHAPTER XV.

TO THE RESCUE.

Diomé had no more information to give. "For the love of life, sir," he entreated, as the brief conference ended, "move off to the other side of the house, or you will be seen by Vanner as he returns. A hunter's eye, Mr. De Brunier, notices the least change in the shadows. You mean to hide among the orchard trees, but you can't stand still. You will be frozen to death, and a moving shadow will betray you."

His cautionary counsels were wasted on a preoccupied mind. De Brunier was examining the fastenings of the door. There was a lock, but the key was with the owners of the hut. There was also a bar which secured it on the inside. Forgill's basket of tools stood by the chimney.

"How much time have we?" asked Mr. De Brunier.

"A good half-hour, sir," replied Diomé.

"Time enough for me to transfer this staple to the outside of the doorpost?"

Diomé hesitated before he answered this inquiry. "Well then?" he asked in turn.

"Well then," repeated Mr. De Brunier, "this Vanner is to meet you here. Don't go out of the hut to take his horse; beckon him to come inside. Shut the door, as if for caution, and tell him you have seen me watching him from the orchard trees. He will listen to that. Two minutes will be enough for me to bar the door on the outside, and we shall have caged the wild hawk before he has had time to pounce upon his prey. I must shut you in together; but play your part well, and leave the rest to me."

"Shut me in with Dick Vanner in a rage!" exclaimed Diomé. "He would smell treachery in a moment. Not for me."

It went hard with Diomé to turn against his old companions. It was clear to Mr. De Brunier the man was afraid of a hand-to-hand encounter. With such half-hearted help the attempt was too hazardous. He changed his tactics.

"I am not in their secrets," protested Diomé. "I am only here to hold his horse. They don't trust me."

"And I," added Mr. De Brunier, "am intent upon preventing mischief. I'll walk round once more. Should you hear the house-door open, you will

112

probably find I have gone in."

Yes, Mr. De Brunier was beginning to regret leaving the house; and yet, if he had not done so, he could not have started Gaspé to intercept the policeman. "Now," he thought, "the boy will be carried off before they can arrive." His thoughts were turning to a probable pursuit. He crossed to the back of the house to look for the Cree. No one better than an Indian for work like that.

The light from the windows of the farm-house was reflected from the shining ground, making it bright as day before them, and deepening the gloom of the shadows beyond. A low, deep growl from Yula brought Mr. De Brunier to the opposite corner of the house, where he discovered Maxica lying on the ground, with his ear to the end of one of the largest logs with which the house was built. They recognized each other instantly, but not a word was said. They were at the angle of the building where the logs crossed each other.

Suddenly Mr. De Brunier remembered the capacity in the uncut trunk of a tree for transmitting sound, and following Maxica's example he too laid his ear to the end of another log, and found himself, as it were, in a whispering gallery. The faintest sound at the other end of the log was distinctly audible. They tried each corner of the house. The music and the dancing from dining-room to kitchen did not detain them long. At the back they could hear the regular breathing of a healthy sleeper and the laboured, painful respiration of the broken-down old man.

The log which crossed the one at which they were now listening ran at the end of the storeroom, and gave back no sound. It was evident both Wilfred and his uncle had fallen asleep, and were therefore off their guard.

To drive up the loose ponies and make them gallop round the house to waken them was a task Yula took off their hands and accomplished so well that Bowkett, listening in the midst of the whirling dancers, believed that Vanner had returned.

Maxica was back at the angle of the logs, moving his ear from one to the other. He raised a warning finger, and laid his ear a little closer to the storeroom side. Mr. De Brunier leaned over him and pressed his own to the tier above. Some one had entered the storeroom.

"Anything here?" asked a low voice.

"What's that behind the door?" whispered another in reply.

113

"A woman's ironing board."

"A woman's what?"

"Never mind what it is if it will slide through the window," interposed a third impatiently, and they were gone.

But the watchers without had heard enough to shape their plan. Maxica was ear, Mr. De Brunier was eye, and so they waited for the first faint echo of the horse-hoofs in the distance or the tinkle of the sledge-bell.

Within the house the merriment ran high. Bridal healths were drank with three times three. The stamp of the untiring dancers drowned the galloping of the ponies.

Aunt Miriam paused a moment, leaning on her bridegroom's arm. "I am dizzy with tiredness," she said. "I think I have danced with every one. I can surely slip away and speak to Caleb now. What made him fasten his door?"

"To keep those travellers out; and now he won't undo it: an old man's crotchet, my dear. I have spoken to him. He is all right, and his cry is, 'Don't disturb me, I must sleep,'" answered Bowkett. "You'll give Batiste his turn? just one more round."

Wilfred was wakened by his Yula's bark beneath the window. Kusky, who was sleeping by the stove, sprang up and answered it, and then crept stealthily to Wilfred's feet.

"That dog will wake the master," said some one in the kitchen.

The bedroom door was softly opened, a low whistle and a tempting bone lured Kusky away. Wilfred was afraid to attempt to detain him, not venturing to show himself to he knew not whom. There was a noise at the window. He remembered it was a double one. It seemed to him somebody was trying to force open the outer pane.

A cry of "Thieves! thieves!" was raised in the kitchen. Wilfred sprang upright. Uncle Caleb wakened with a groan.

"Look to the door. Guard every window," shouted Bowkett, rushing into the room, followed by half-a-dozen of his friends, who had seized their guns as they ran.

The outer window was broken. Through the inner, which was not so thickly frozen, Wilfred could see the shadow of a man. He knew that Bowkett was by the side of the bed, but his eyes were fixed on the pane.

114

At the first smash of the butt end of Vanner's gun, through shutter and frame, Mr. De Brunier laid a finger on Maxica's arm. The Cree, who was holding down Yula, suddenly let him go with a growl and a spring. Vanner half turned his head, but Yula's teeth were in his collar. The thickness of the hunter's clothing kept the grip from his throat, but he was dragged backwards. Maxica knelt upon him in a moment, with a huge stone upraised, ready to dash his brains out if he ventured to utter a cry. Mr. De Brunier stepped out from the shadow and stood before the window, waiting in Vanner's stead. For what? He hardly dared to think. The window was raised a finger's breadth, and the muzzle of a hunter's gun was pointed at his ear. He drew a little aside and flattened himself against the building. The gun was fired into the air.

"That is a feint," thought Mr. De Brunier. "They have not seen us yet. When they do, the tug comes. Two against twenty at the very least, unless we hear the sledge-bell first. It is a question of time. The clock is counting life and death for more than one of us. All hinges on my Gaspé. Thank God, I know he will do his very best. There is no mistrust of Gaspé; and if I fall before he comes, if I meet death in endeavouring to rescue this fatherless boy, the God who sees it all, in whose hand these lawless hunters are but as grasshoppers, will never forget my Gaspé."

The report of Bowkett's gun roused old Caleb's latent fire.

"What is it?" he demanded. "Are the Indians upon us? Where is Miriam?"

Wilfred threw the bearskin across his feet over the old man's back.

"I am here!" cried Bowkett, with an ostentatious air of protection. "I'll defend the place; but the attack is at this end of the house. First of all, I carry you to Miriam and safety at the other."

Bowkett, in the full pride of his strength, lifted up the feeble old man as if he were a child and carried him out of the room.

"Wilfred, my boy, keep close to me, keep close," called Uncle Caleb; but a strong man's hand seized hold of Wilfred and pulled him back.

"Who are you?" demanded Wilfred, struggling with all his might. "Let me go, I tell you; let me go!"

The door was banged up behind Uncle Caleb and Bowkett. The room was full of men.

Wilfred knew too well the cry of "Thieves" was all humbug—a sham to get him away from his uncle.

115

"Forgill! Forgill!" he shouted. "Pête! Pête! Help me! help me!"

A pillow was tossed in his face.

"Don't cram the little turkey-cock with his own feathers," said a voice he was almost glad to recognize, for he could not feel that Mathurin would really hurt him. He kicked against his captor, and getting one hand free, he tried to grasp at this possible friend; but the corner of the pillow, crushed into his mouth, choked his shouts. "So it's Mathurin's own old babby, is it?" continued the deep, jovial voice. "Didn't I tell ye he was uncommon handy with his little fists? But he is a regular mammy's darling for all that. It is Mathurin will put the pappoose in its cradle. Ah! but if it won't lie still, pat it on its little head; Batiste can show you how."

In all this nonsense Wilfred comprehended the threat and the caution. His frantic struggles were useless. They only provoked fresh bursts of merriment. Oh, it was hard to know they were useless, and feel the impotency of his rage! He was forced to give in. They bound him in the sheets.

Mathurin was shouting for—

> "A rabbit-skin,
> To wrap his baby bunting in.

They took the rug from the floor and wrapped it round Wilfred. He was laid on the ironing board.

He felt the strong, firm straps that were binding him to it growing tighter and tighter.

What were they going to do with him? and where was Mr. De Brunier?

The hunters set him up against the wall, like the pappoose in the wigwam of the Blackfoot chief, whilst they opened the window.

Mr. De Brunier stood waiting, his arms uplifted before his face, ready to receive the burden they were to let fall. It was but a little bit of face that was ever visible beneath a Canadian fur cap, such as both the men were wearing. Smoked skin was the only clothing which could resist the climate, therefore the sleeves of one man's coat were like the sleeves of another. The noisy group in the bedroom, who had been drinking healths all night, saw little but the outstretched arms, and took no notice.

"Young lambs to sell!" shouted Mathurin, heaving up the board.

116

"What if he takes to blaring?" said one of the others.

"Let him blare as he likes when once he is outside," retorted a third.

"Lull him off with 'Yankee-doodle,'" laughed another.

"He'll just lie quiet like a little angel, and then nothing will hurt him," continued the incorrigible Mathurin, "till we come to—

"'Hush-a-bye, baby, on the tree-top,
When the wind blows the cradle will rock;
When the bough breaks the cradle will fall,
Then down goes cradle, and baby, and all.'"

This ridiculous nursery ditty, originated by the sight of the Indian pappooses hung so often on the bough of a tree when their mothers are busy, read to Wilfred his doom.

Would these men really take him out into the darksome forest, and hang him to some giant pine, and leave him there, as Pe-na-Koam was left, to die alone of hunger and cold?

It was an awful moment. The end of the board to which he was bound was resting on the window-sill.

"Gently now," said one.

"Steady there," retorted another.

"Now it is going beautifully," cried a third.

"Ready, Vanner, ready," they exclaimed in chorus. Caution and prudence had long since gone to the winds with the greater part of them. Mathurin alone kept the control.

Mr. De Brunier nodded, and placed himself between the window and the two men on the snow in deadly silent wrestle, trusting that his own dark shadow might screen them from observation yet a little longer. He saw Wilfred's feet appear at the window. His hand was up to guide the board in a moment, acting in concert with the men above. They slid it easily to the ground.

Mr. De Brunier's foot was on a knot in the logs of the wall, and stretching upwards he shut the window from the outside. It was beyond his power to fasten it; but a moment or two were gained. His knife was soon hacking at the straps which bound Wilfred to his impromptu cradle. They looked in

117

each other's faces; not a word was breathed. Wilfred's hands were freed. He sat up and drew out his feet from the thick folds of the rug. Mr. De Brunier seized his hand, and they ran, as men run for their lives, straight to Forgill's hut.

Diomé saw them coming. He was still leading Vanner's horse. He wheeled it round and covered their retreat, setting it off prancing and curvetting between them and the house.

Through the open door of Forgill's hut the fire was glowing like a beacon across the snow. It was the darkest hour of all that brilliant night. The moon was sinking low, the stars were fading; the dawning was at hand.

The hut was gained at last. The door was shut behind the fugitives, and instantly barred. Every atom of furniture the hut contained was piled against it, and then they listened for the return of the sledge. Whether daylight would increase their danger or diminish it, Mr. De Brunier hardly knew. But with the dreaded daylight came the faint tinkle of a distant bell and the jingling of a chain bridle.

The Canadian police in the Dominion of the far North-West are an experienced troop of cavalry. Trooper and charger are alike fitted for the difficult task of maintaining law and order among the scattered, lawless population sprinkling its vast plains and forest wilds. No bronco can outride the splendid war-horse, and the mere sight of his scarlet-coated rider produces an effect which we in England little imagine. For he is the representative of the strong and even hand of British justice, which makes itself felt wherever it touches, ruling all alike with firmness and mercy, exerting a moral force to which even the Blackfoot in his moya yields.

Mr. De Brunier pulled down his barricade almost before it was finished, for the sledge came shooting down the clearing with the policeman behind it.

Wilfred clasped his hands together at the joyful sight. "They come! they come!" he cried.

Out ran Mr. De Brunier, waving his arms in the air to attract attention, and direct the policeman to the back of the farm-house, where he had left Dick Vanner writhing under Maxica's grasp on the frozen ground.

When the window was so suddenly closed from the outside, the hunters, supposing Vanner had shut it, let it alone for a few minutes, until wonder prompted Mathurin to open it just a crack for a peep-hole.

118

At the sight of Vanner held down by his Indian antagonist he threw it to its widest. Gun after gun was raised and pointed at Maxica's head; but none of them dared to fire, for the ball would have struck Vanner also. Mathurin was leaping out of the window to his assistance, when Yula relaxed his hold of Vanner's collar, and sprang at Mathurin, seizing him by the leg, and keeping him half in half out of the window, so that no one else could get out over him or release him from the inside.

There was a general rush to the porch; but the house-door had been locked and barred by Bowkett's orders, and the key was in his pocket.

He did it to prevent any of the Aclands' old servants going out of the house to interfere with Vanner. It was equally successful in keeping in the friends who would have gone to his help.

"The key! the key!" roared Batiste.

Another seized on old Pête and shook him because he would not open the door. In vain Pête protested the key was missing. They were getting furious. "The key! the key!" was reiterated in an ever-increasing crescendo.

They seized on Pête and shook him again. They would have the key.

Mathurin's yell for help grew more desperate. With one hand holding on to the window-frame, he could not beat off the dog. The blows he aimed at him with the other were uncertain and feeble.

"Who let the brute out?" demanded Batiste.

He had seen Yula lying by the kitchen fire when he first arrived, and of course knew him again. Ah! and the dog had recognized him also, for he had saluted him with a low, deep growl. It had watched its chance. It was paying back old scores. Batiste knew that well.

Another howl of pain from Mathurin.

The heel of an English boot might have given such a kick under the lock that it would have sent the spring back with a jerk; but they were all wearing the soft, glove-like moccasin, and knew no more about the mechanism of a lock than a baby. Their life had been passed in the open; when they left the saddle for the hut in the winter camp, their ideas of door-fastening never rose beyond the latch and the bar. A dozen gun-stocks battered on the door. It was tough and strong, and never stirred.

Pête was searching everywhere for the key. He would have let them out gladly, only too thankful to rid the house of such a noisy crew, and leave

119

them to fight the thieves outside; but no key was to be found.

"We always hang it on this nail," he protested, groping about the floor.

Patience could hold out no longer. There was a shout for Bowkett.

"Don't leave me," Miriam had entreated, when Bowkett brought her brother into the dining-room and set him in the arm-chair by the fire; for she thought the old man's life would go every moment, and Forgill shared her fears.

"There are enough to defend the place," he said, "without me;" and he gave all his care to his master.

"The boy! Wilfred!" gasped Caleb Acland, making vain attempts to return to find him. His sister and Forgill thought he was wandering, and trusted in Bowkett's strong arm to hold him back.

How could Bowkett leave his bride? He was keeping his hands clean. There were plenty to do his dirty work. He himself was to have nothing to do with it, according to Vanner's programme. He would not go.

CHAPTER XVI.

IN CONFUSION.

There was a thundering rap at the dining-room window, and a voice Bowkett instantly recognized as Diomé's rang out the warning word,—

"The police! The police are here!"

"Thank God!" exclaimed Miriam; but her bridegroom's cheek grew deadly pale, and he rushed into the kitchen, key in hand. The clamouring group around the door divided before him, as Diomé hissed his warning through the keyhole.

The door flew open. Bowkett was almost knocked down by his hurrying guests. Each man for his horse. Some snatched up their guns, some left them behind. Broncos were caught by the mane, by the ear, by the tail. Their masters sprang upon their backs. Each man leaped upon the first horse he could lay hold of, saddle or no saddle, bridle or no bridle. What did it matter so that they got away? or else, horrors of horrors! such an escapade as they had been caught in might get one or other among them shut up for a month or two in Garry Jail. They scattered in every direction, as chickens scatter at the flutter of the white owl's wing.

Diomé put the bridle of Vanner's horse into Bowkett's hand. "To the frontier," he whispered. "You know the shortest road. We are parting company; for I go northwards."

Bowkett looked over his shoulder to where Pête stood staring in the doorway. "Tell your mistress we are starting in pursuit," he shouted, loud enough for all to hear, as he sprang on Vanner's horse and galloped off, following the course of the wild geese to Yankee land.

Within ten minutes after the first jingling sound from the light shake of the trooper's bridle the place was cleared.

"Oh, I did it!" said Gaspé, with his arm round Wilfred's neck. "I was back to a minute, wasn't I, grandfather?"

Mr. De Brunier scarcely waited to watch the break-neck flight. He was off with the sledge-driver to the policeman's assistance. He beckoned to the boys to follow him at a cautious distance, judging it safer than leaving them unguarded in Forgill's hut.

The policeman, seeing Yula had already arrested Mathurin, turned to the two on the ground. He knocked the stone out of Maxica's hand, and handcuffed Vanner.

Mr. De Brunier was giving his evidence on the spot. "I was warned there would be mischief here before morning. I sent my messenger for you, and watched the house all night. The Indian and the dog were with me. I saw this fellow attempt to break in at that window. The dog flew on him, dragged him to the ground, and the Indian held him there. That other man I denounce as an accomplice indoors, evidently acting in concert with him."

Wilfred shook off Gaspé's arm and flew to Yula. "Leave go," he said, "leave go." His hands went round the dog's throat to enforce obedience as he whispered, "I am not quite a babby to choke him off like that, am I? Draw your leg up, Mathurin, and run. You meant to save me—I saw it in your face—and I'll save you. The porch-door stands open, run!"

Mathurin drew up his leg with a groan, but Yula's teeth had gone so deeply into the flesh he could scarcely move for pain. If Mathurin could not run, the sledge-driver could. He was round the house and through the porch before Mathurin could reach it. He collared him by the kitchen-table, to Pête's amazement. Forgill burst out of the dining-room, ready to identify him as one of their guests, and was pushed aside. The policeman was dragging in his prisoner.

Mr. De Brunier held Wilfred by the arm. "You should not have done that," he was saying. "Your dog knew what he was about better than you did. At any other time to call him off would only have been humane and right, but in such circumstances—"

He never finished his sentence. There was Mathurin cowed and trembling at the sight of Yula, who was marching into the porch with his head up and his tail wagging in triumph.

Aunt Miriam, aghast and pale, stood in the doorway of the dining-room. Mr. De Brunier led her aside for a word of explanation. "The thieves among the guests of her wedding party, incredible!" She was stunned.

Yula seated himself in front of Mathurin, daring him to move hand or foot.

Wilfred was looking round him for the Cree, who was feeling for his bow and arrows, thrown somewhere on the ground during his prolonged struggle. When the stone was struck from Maxica's grasp, and he knew that Vanner was dragged off helpless, he felt himself in the presence of a power that was mightier than his own. As Wilfred caught up the bow and put it in his hand, he said solemnly, "You are safe under the shadow of that great white warrior chief, and Maxica is no longer needed; for as the horse is as seven to the dog, so is the great white medicine as seven to one, therefore the redman shuns his presence, and here we part."

"Not yet, not yet," urged Wilfred desperately; but whilst he was speaking the Cree was gone. He had vanished with the morning shadows behind the pine trees.

Wilfred stretched out his arms to recall him; but Gaspé, who had followed his friend like his shadow, pulled him back. "It would be but poor gratitude for Maxica's gallant rescue to run your head into the noose a second time," he said. "With these hunters lurking about the place, we ought to make our way indoors as fast as we can."

The chill of the morning wrapped them round. They were shivering in the icy mist, through which the rising sun was struggling. It was folly to linger. Gaspé knew the Indian was afraid to trust himself in the company of the policeman.

"Shall I never see him more?" burst out Wilfred mournfully.

"Don't say that," retorted Gaspé. "He is sure to come again to Hungry Hall with the furs from his winter's hunting. You can meet him then."

"I? I shall be at school at Garry. How can I go there?" asked Wilfred.

"At Garry," repeated his consoler, brightening. "Well, from Garry you can send him anything you like by the winter packet of letters. You know our postman, the old Indian, who carries them in his dog-sled to every one of the Hudson Bay stations. You can send what you like by him to Hungry Hall. Sooner or later it will be sure to reach your dusky friend."

"It will be something to let him know I don't forget," sighed Wilfred, whose foot was in his uncle's porch, where safety was before him.

There was a sudden stillness about the place. A kind of paralysis had seized upon the household, as it fell under the startling interdict of the policeman: "Not a thing on the premises to be touched; not an individual to leave them until he gave permission." This utter standstill was more appalling to the farm-servants than the riotous confusion which had preceded it. The dread of what would come next lay like a nightmare over master and men.

Wilfred scarcely looked at prisoners or policeman; he made his way to his uncle.

"I can finish my prayer this morning, and I will—I will try to do my duty. Tell me what it is?"

"To speak the truth," returned old Caleb solemnly, "without fear or prevarication. No, no! don't tell me beforehand what you are going to say, or that fellow in the scarlet coat will assert I have tutored you."

Gaspé began to speak.

"No, no!" continued Uncle Caleb, "you must not talk it over with your friend. Sit down, my boy; think of all that has happened in the night quietly and calmly, and God help us to bear the result."

Again he rocked himself backwards and forwards, murmuring under his breath, "My poor Miriam! I have two to think of—my poor, poor Miriam!"

Wilfred's own clear commonsense came to his aid; he looked up brightly. The old man's tears were slowly trickling down his furrowed cheeks. "Uncle," he urged, "my friends have not only saved me, they have saved you all. They stopped those fellows short, before they had time to do their worst. They will not be punished for what they were going to do, but for what they actually did do."

123

A sudden rush of gratitude came over Wilfred as he recalled his peril. His arms went round Gaspé with a clasp that seemed to know no unloosening. A friend is worth all hazards.

His turn soon came. Aunt Miriam had preceded her nephew. She had so little to tell. "In the midst of the dancing there was a cry of 'Thieves!' The men ran. Her husband came back to her, bringing her invalid brother to the safest part of the house. He stayed to guard them, until there arose a second cry, 'The police!' She supposed the thieves made off. Her husband had started in pursuit."

In pursuit, when there was nothing to pursue; the aggressor was already taken. Aunt Miriam saw the inevitable inference: her husband had fled with his guests. She never looked up. She could not meet the eyes around her, until she was asked if Vanner and Mathurin were among her guests. Her pale cheeks grew paler.

Their own men were stupid and sleepy, and could only stare at each other. All they had had to say confirmed their mistress's statements.

Mr. De Brunier had fetched Wilfred whilst his aunt was speaking. He looked at the men crowding round the table, pushed between the sledge-driver and Pête to where his aunt was standing, and squeezed her hand. There was just one look exchanged between them. Of all the startling events in that strange night, it was strangest of all to Aunt Miriam to see him there. The fervency in the pressure she returned set Wilfred's heart at ease. One determination possessed them both—not to make a scene.

Aunt Miriam got back into her own room; how, she never knew. She threw herself on her knees beside her bed, and listened; for in that wood-built house every word could be heard as plainly as if she had remained in the kitchen. Her grief and shame were hidden, that was all.

Wilfred's clear, straightforward answers made it plain there were no thieves in the case. Her wedding guests had set upon her little wanderer in the moment of his return.

Vanner, scowling and sullen, never uttered a single word.

Mathurin protested volubly. He never meant to let them hurt the boy, but some amongst them owed him a grudge, and they were bent on paying it off before they parted.

"A base and cowardly trick, by your own showing, to break into an old man's room in the dead of the night with a false alarm; not to mention

124

your behaviour to the boy. If this outrage hastens the old gentleman's end, you will find yourselves in a very awkward position. His seizure in the night was solely due to the unwarrantable alarm," observed the policeman.

Mathurin began to interrupt. He checked him.

"If you have anything to say for yourself, reserve it for the proper time and place; for the present you must step into that sledge and come with me at once.—Mr. De Brunier, I shall meet you and your son at Garry on the twenty-ninth."

He marched his prisoners through the porch; a sullen silence reigned around. The sledge-bell tinkled, the snow gleamed white as ever in the morning sunshine, as Vanner and Mathurin left the farm.

With the air of a mute at a funeral, Forgill bolted the door behind them. Mr. De Brunier walked into the sleeping-room, to examine the scene of confusion it presented for himself.

Aunt Miriam came out, leaving the door behind her open, without knowing it. She moved like one in a dream. "I cannot understand all this," she said, "but we must do the thing that is nearest."

She directed Forgill to board up the broken window and to see that the house was secure, and took Pête with her to make up a bed for her brother in the dining-room. She laid her hand on Wilfred's shoulder as she passed him, but the words died on her lips.

The men obeyed her without reply. Forgill was afraid to go out of the house alone. As the cowman followed him, he patted Yula's head, observing, "After all that's said and done, it was this here dog which caught 'em. I reckon he's worth his weight in gold, wherever he comes from, that I do."

Yula shook off the stranger's caress as if it were an impertinent freedom. His eye was fixed on two small moccasined feet peeping out from under Aunt Miriam's bed.

There was a spring, but Wilfred's hand was in his collar.

"I know I had better stop him," he whispered, looking up at Gaspé, as he thought of Mr. De Brunier's reproof.

"Right enough now," cried Gaspé. "Wilfred, it is a girl."

He ran to the bed and handed out Bowkett's young sister, Anastasia. Her dress was of the universal smoked skin, but its gay embroidery of beads and the white ribbons which adorned it spoke of the recent bridal. Her black hair fell in one long, heavy braid to her waist.

"Oh, you uncomplimentary creatures!" she exclaimed, "not one of you remembered my existence; but I'll forgive you two"—extending a hand to each—"because you did not know of it. I crawled in here at the first alarm, and here I have lain trembling, and nobody missed me. But, I declare, you men folk have been going on awful. You will be the death of us all some of these days. I could have knocked your heads together until I had knocked some sense into you. Put your pappoose in its cradle, indeed! I wish you were all pappooses; I would soon let you know what I think of upsetting a poor old man like that."

The indignant young beauty shook the dust from her embroidery, and twirled her white ribbons into their places as she spoke.

"Spoiling all the fun," she added.

"Now don't perform upon us, Miss Bowkett," put in Gaspé. "We are not the representatives of last night's rowdyism. My poor friend here is chief sufferer from it. Only he had a four-footed friend, and a dark-skinned friend, and two others at the back of them of a very ordinary type, but still friends with hands and feet. So the tables were turned, and the two real representatives are gone up for their exam."

"I daren't be the first to tell a tale like this in the hunters' camp. Besides," she demanded, "who is to take me there? This is what the day after brings," she pouted, passing the boys as she went into the kitchen. The guns which the hunters had left behind them had been carefully unloaded by the policeman and Mr. De Brunier, and were piled together in one corner, waiting for their owners to reclaim them. Every one knew the hunters could not live without their trading guns; they must come back to fetch them. Anastasia, too, was aware she had only to wait for the first who should put in an appearance to escort her home. Little was said, for Aunt Miriam knew Anastasia's departure from Acland's Hut would be Hugh Bowkett's recall.

When Mr. De Brunier understood this, his anxiety on Wilfred's account was redoubled.

But when Uncle Caleb revived enough for conversation, he spoke of the little business to be settled between them, and asked for Mr. De Brunier.

"I have thought it all through," he said. "In the face of the Cree's warning,

126

and all that happened under this roof, I can never leave my nephew and Hugh Bowkett to live together beneath it. As soon as he hears from his sister how matters stand here, and finds sentence has been passed on Vanner and Mathurin, he may come back at any hour. I want to leave my nephew to your care; a better friend he could not have."

"As he has had it already, he shall always have it, as if he were next to Gaspé, I promise you," was the ready answer.

"I want a little more than that," Uncle Caleb continued. "I want you to take him away at once, and send him back to school. You spoke of buying land; buy half of mine. That will be Wilfred's portion. Invest the money in the Hudson Bay Company, where Bowkett can never touch it, and I shall feel my boy is safe. As for Miriam, she will still have a good home and a good farm; and the temptation out of his reach, Bowkett may settle down."

"I have no faith in bribery for making a man better. It wants the change here, and that is God's work, not man's," returned Mr. De Brunier, tapping his own breast.

Caleb Acland had but one more charge: "Let nobody tell poor Miriam the worst." But she knew enough without the telling.

When Wilfred found he was to return to Garry with his friends the next day his arms went round his dogs, and a look of mute appeal wandered from Mr. De Brunier to Aunt Miriam.

"Had not I better take back Kusky?" suggested Gaspé. "And could not we have Yula too?"

"Yula!" repeated Aunt Miriam. "It is I who must take care of Yula. He shall never want a bone whilst I have one. I shall feed him, Wilfred, with my own hands till you come back to claim him."

THE END.

Printed in Great Britain
by Amazon